The Hideaway

**(hardcover title:
The Hideaway Summer)**

by BEVERLY HOLLETT RENNER

*inside illustrations by Ruth Sanderson
cover by Fran Stiles*

SCHOLASTIC BOOK SERVICES

NEW YORK • TORONTO • LONDON • AUCKLAND • SYDNEY • TOKYO

For my family,
most particularly,
Dick, Sherrie, Amy, Paul

ISBN 0-590-31308-8

Text copyright © 1978 by Beverly Hollett Renner. Illustrations copyright © 1978 by Ruth Sanderson. All rights reserved. This edition is published by Scholastic Book Services, a division of Scholastic Magazines, Inc., 50 West 44th Street, New York, New York 10036, by arrangement with Harper & Row Publishers, Inc.

12 11 10 9 8 7 6 5 4 3 2 1   4   0 1 2 3 4 5/8
Printed in the U.S.A.   06

One

Addie Carver would forever deny planning what happened. The bus leaned around the last curve before Groten's Crossroads Grocery, and...

"Before I knew it, my hand simply grabbed that cord and yanked hard twice."

She would admit, however, that once the buzzers sounded, she did not hesitate to act.

Quickly, she shook her little brother. His head had been resting on her shoulder.

"Come on, Clay. We're getting off here."

Clay blinked. "This camp?"

"No, it's Gram's corner. Hurry up. You take the duffel bag."

"But Addie, why...?"

"I'm taking you to The Riffles. Back to see The Hideaway."

Clay's eyes grew round.

"Come on, Clay. We can catch the next bus in a couple of hours. Hurry now, or I'm going to leave you."

She didn't mean it, but being firm had proved to be the best way to halt tears or further questions.

The bus pulled off the highway and lurched to a stop in the sparsely graveled parking area in front of the store. Addie led the way, balanced by a suitcase in each hand. Clay stumbled sleepily after her, dragging the duffel bag. They watched the bus disappear around the next curve, taking its noise with it.

"Hey, Addie..." Clay tugged at her sleeve, but she shook him off. She tilted her head with eyes half closed, listening, inhaling deeply.

A single crow squawked overhead. Insects hummed in the tangle of honeysuckle that leaned against the unpainted fence next to the store. From somewhere beyond the bridge came the fluttering sound of motors—tractors coming and going in the fields. "That's hay. That wonderful smell is freshly cut hay." Addie sighed with pleasure. She had been so miserable on the bus. How could she ride on by to Camp Witchetee as if this corner meant nothing?

Every summer since Dad and Gram Carver

had thought she was old enough to ride the bus alone, she'd pulled the cord two times at the last curve before Groten's Crossroads Grocery. The bus would pull over and the doors fold back to show Gram standing—right here—ready to swoop her off the steps in a hug. But not this summer. Not ever again.

Here she stood with Clay, a nine-year-old brother she hardly knew. Mother was in Europe, remarried after all these years; Dad, as usual in the summer, was at a construction site; and Gram, Gram was dead. Addie was left all alone.

"Addie?" There was another tug at her sleeve. "Are we really going to see The Hideaway?"

"Sure, Clay."

He was excited. Since he'd come to live with them, her tales about The Hideaway and how they were going to fix it up had become his bedtime stories.

Addie had told him how when Dad was a boy and Grandpa Carver was still living, they'd hauled the big oak shed through the woods without breaking one pane of glass. The front of it was made up almost entirely of windows. They'd turned the shed to overlook The Riffles at the bend just beyond the sandbar. Then they'd jacked it up on concrete blocks and built steps to the door on the side.

Through the years, they'd added a water pump and sink and moved in a potbellied stove. A wide bench, stretching the full width of the shed, had been tucked cozily against the rear wall under the sharply slanting roof. Addie didn't know what Dad had used the bench for, but whenever she played there, she'd pretended it was her bed.

The shed had been Dad's secret clubhouse, known only to his best friend. For Addie, it had started as a playhouse furnished with cast-off chairs, chipped dishes and apple crates from the farm. It became other things as the summers went by — a ship, space station, alpine hut, pioneer cabin. Then she grew older, and tired of the pretend games and just used the shed as a quiet place.

At the end of last summer, when it was too late to do much about it, she saw what the shed could really be — a retreat on the river, a cottage in the woods — with just a little fixing up.

"We can do it, Gram. Some paint, maybe some old curtains. We can fix it up so we can stay there if we want."

Gram had said, "We'll see."

But with Gram that almost always meant yes. Addie had begun making plans and had painted a sign that Dad helped her nail above the door the morning he came to take her home. The letters spelled it clearly. The old shed was christened The Hideaway, a proper name for a place on the river. But that's all that had been done to make it so, except for plans she'd made through the winter, plans that could never come true.

"Hey, Addie, aren't we going to go?"

"Yes, sure we are."

There were still no cars in sight. As far as she knew no one had seen them. She hadn't noticed any movement behind the dingy windows of the store. They could leave their suitcases there, but she didn't feel like making explanations to Mrs. Groten. Besides, the suitcases weren't that heavy and it wasn't that far.

"Come on, Clay."

Addie hitched up the suitcases and started toward the blacktop road that ran alongside the store. They would take it as far as The River Road just beyond the bridge.

Clay swung the duffel bag over his shoulder, teetering a bit under its weight, and fell into step behind her. She could count on his following her. He stuck to her like a burr most of the time. Once, when she'd complained about it to Dad, he'd laughed.

"Now, Addie, you can't blame him for being a bit of a momma's boy — that's all he's known."

Addie had wanted to answer, "But *I'm* not his momma," but she hadn't. It had been hard for Clay moving to a new town, starting a new school and getting used to a father and sister all at once.

He'd been a baby when Mother had taken him to live with her in New York City right after the divorce. Addie had been three years old, and as the older had stayed with Dad in the duplex in Indianapolis. Both parents had wanted them, so this had been the only fair way. As the baby, Clay had needed to be with Mother.

However, after Mother married the Air Force colonel, everyone agreed it would be better for Clay to move in with Dad and Addie. Moving was something Addie had never done: Summers at the farm with Gram, winters at home was the way it had always been.

Going to camp was a new experience for her, too, but Dad didn't seem to worry about that. The last words he'd said as they boarded the bus that morning had been to Clay: "Stick with Addie. She'll know what to do."

Wonder what Dad would think if he knew they weren't going directly to camp? He'd been so proud of finding out about Camp Witchetee.

"You'll love it, Addie," Dad had said, "and Clay, it'll be good for you to learn about the outdoors."

She hadn't told Dad that Clay had cried himself to sleep last night. After all, where else could they go on such short notice for a whole summer? But it was going to be hard on Clay—another new place, more strangers, so soon.

Addie thought they could stop at the bridge and look at the river, but when she realized the guardrail was too high for Clay to peek over, she kept going. The suitcases were getting heavy, but Clay was keeping up so well she didn't call a stop until they turned onto The River Road.

"I've got to rest a minute," she said, dropping the suitcases and sitting down on one.

Clay let the duffel bag slide off his shoulder, but didn't sit on the suitcase she offered him. He looked up into the row of walnut trees they'd stopped under, then back to the bridge as if afraid he'd missed something. Then, suddenly, he pointed ahead on down the gravel road.

"There! Where The River Road turns — that's The Riffles, isn't it? Where it begins? I can see the big trees you said grow next to the meadow."

Addie nodded. Yes, there it was — just the same — the fringe of treetops that marked the beginning of Carver land. The Riffles, the forty acres that edged the river, was all that was left now of the farm. Dad had sold the rest right after the funeral.

"No one wants The Riffles," he'd told Addie. "They all think of it as floodplain and wilderness. But you know, I sure had a lot of fun there when I was a kid, and I think it was your grandmother's favorite part of the whole farm."

Addie knew it was. Her earliest memory of Gram Carver was in the meadow at The Riffles. Addie had stood, surrounded by swaying black-eyed Susans almost as tall as she was. Gram had leaned over, putting a finger to her lips, and then had gently lifted a branch on a low bush. There had been a perfect nest, a song sparrow's nest, with three tiny heads bobbing like the flowers around them.

Addie was woozily sick with flu when the

word came that Gram had died in her sleep. Dad went alone to the funeral. Now, looking ahead to The Riffles, it was hard to believe that Gram was gone. Everything looked the same.

"Shouldn't we be going?" Clay asked.

Addie nodded again and slowly picked up the suitcases. Clay swung the duffel bag back into place and started down the road. Addie let him keep the lead. The suitcases seemed heavier, but then, there was a heaviness within her, too. If she walked slow enough, maybe she could recapture it all — keep it the same — for just a little longer.

But, wasn't it the same? As always, the grass alongside The River Road was powdered white from gravel dust. Squirrels scolded at them from the branches above. Clay was surprised, but she wasn't, when a red-headed woodpecker swooped ahead and landed on a telephone pole.

"I've never seen a real one," he called back.

Addie didn't tell him there had always been at least one red-headed woodpecker along here. He was enjoying it, being in the lead, making his discoveries, but she was ready to move ahead of him again when they left the road at the bend. The barbed-wire fence needed to be crawled through first, and she wasn't sure Clay had ever seen one up close before.

"Here," she said, poking the biggest suitcase between the middle and bottom wires to widen the gap. "Duck through here."

Clay threw the duffel bag over first, then slid past the wires without a snag. Addie followed quickly. They were standing now in the thicket of wild roses, hawthorn, and locust that edged the fence line, a thicket of thorns.

Addie held the suitcases in front of her like a shield.

"Let me go first," she said, "but stay close behind."

Gram had not minded the thicket. She had claimed that it was better than the fence for keeping out hunters.

As they came out under the big trees, the thicket gave way to oak and beech seedlings. The meadow was just ahead. It, too, Addie could see, was the same. Dressed properly for June, the meadow was bowing and waving white and purple with daisies and clover.

Clay ran ahead once more, cutting a path through the grass as he headed straight for the bend where the river came out of the woods. Addie was not surprised when he stopped short as he got his first look.

It was no ordinary river. Its source was an underground spring just across the Ohio border. Flowing westward into Indiana, it wound and curved gracefully through fields edged by woods. As it neared the forty acres of The Riffles, the river began to wind and twist almost back upon itself in places. The surrounding woodlands thickened and deepened.

At The Riffles, the river is shallow and clear. The bottom is limestone, scattered with rocks that layer themselves like loose cobblestone streets, or tumble along to collect into piles forming the rocky shoals that are called riffles.

Clay had thought she'd said "ripples" when she'd told him about them.

"The water may 'ripple' as it goes over the riffles," she'd explained, "but riffles are the rocky shoals themselves."

They appear in many places along the river, but nowhere are there so many riffles so close together as at The Riffles. Although the river moves through flat, eastern Indiana farmland, it is not unlike a wide mountain stream. Except when muddied by runoff from freshly plowed fileds, the water is pure enough to drink and clear enough to watch the fish swimming or the crayfish jet-propelling themselves from rock to rock along the bottom.

11

Sweat ran down Addie's face and back. If it hadn't been for the suitcases, she would have waded in and walked the rest of the way to The Hideway in the cool bubbling water.

Instead, she moved on to find the path she knew would be there. Fishermen had made it along the bank as far as the sandbar at the next bend. It stopped there. No one, it seemed, wanted to walk farther back into the woods.

Addie found it strange that grown men were uneasy about woodlands when she felt so at home there. She loved the smell, so fresh, and the quiet; and yet, there was always movement to remind her that she was not alone.

Clay tugged once more at her sleeve. His eyes were shining as he leaned close to whisper, "It's like a different world in here under the trees, a secret place, isn't it?"

Addie looked up to the canopy of tree branches still lacy with early summer. Soon the canopy would thicken, weaving a solid cover.

Did Clay feel the same snugness she did, safe and welcome in here? She knew the answer and it made her flush with anger, anger at herself. What had she done? What good was this — bringing him to The Riffles and taking him to The Hideaway?

What good was it doing *her* to see it all again? They would just have to leave it. They should have stayed on the bus. This was only making it more difficult. Nothing was going to be the same really — not ever again.

Still, she stumbled on. Any other time she would have walked the length of the fallen tree in the path or stopped to swing on the wild grapevines. Clay saw them and soon began to fall behind. Finally, Addie stopped to wait. As Clay came near again, she said flatly, "The Hideaway's around the next bend."

"It *is*?" Clay hurried forward. His eagerness was like a slap. Addie dropped the suitcases.

"Just a minute, Clay. I don't know what you expect. I told you about The Hideaway. It's just a big, old unpainted shed, that's all."

But even as she spoke, Clay moved past her, hurrying around the bend.

"Hey, Addie," he called. "I see it. I see The Hideaway. It looks great! Like brand new!"

Two

The Hideaway wasn't brand new, but the only thing that looked the same was the sign Addie had nailed above the door last summer.

From its shake-shingled rooftop to the freshly painted concrete blocks it stood on, it had been renewed. The weather-gray boards that had never been painted were stained a soft forest green. All the trim, the door and the steps had been painted white. At the front, the windows were underlined now by a window box, ready to be planted with flowers.

The Hideaway wasn't a shed. It was a summer cottage, a retreat on the river.

"Oh, Gram, Gram." Addie reached for Clay's arm. "She's fixed it all up, don't you see? Gram's fixed it all up for us."

14

Addie hurried forward, stumbling up the steps and groping above the door to open the padlock. The key was there, but her hands trembled so, Clay was beside her before she could wiggle it into the lock. It worked easily. It had been oiled just a few weeks ago.

Addie pulled the door open. There was a screen door. There had never been one before. Slowly Addie pushed it aside.

"Clay. Look! Just look!"

The walls and ceiling were painted white, but everything else was color, like Gram's flower bed in full bloom. Bright yellow draperies in an old-fashioned calico print hung on big brass rings to frame the windows. There were shelves above the sink and cupboards below it and a bookcase next to the door painted in glossy red, yellow and blue.

The bench that Addie had pretended was a bed had become one. The bright calico covering it now was so puffed, so plumped, that Addie knew it must be layered with a mattress from Gram's feather bed. She ran to jump on it, sinking into its softness. Large square pillows of red, yellow and blue were propped along the wall behind her. They billowed around her as she fell back into them.

"Oh, Clay, isn't this fantastic?" She popped

up again and opened a big drawer under the bed.

Clay had been standing in the doorway watching Addie, but he hurried forward when she spoke to touch the trundle bed with his fingertips, and then with one quick movement he turned, sprang into the air and plopped full-length backwards onto his feather bed. A slow smile spread across his face.

Addie ran to the table and chairs next to the windows.

"Look, Clay. You can sit right here and look out over the river while you eat. This is Gram's old kitchen table. She's refinished it — and the chairs, too."

Gently, Addie touched the kerosene lamp in the center of the table. She ran her fingers along the graceful glass chimney and then down over the carved glass base.

"I know this lamp. This is our great-grandmother's very own lamp. Gram showed it to me."

Addie turned again. There was a rocking chair on an oval braided rug near the pot-bellied stove in the middle of the room.

"And this is Gram's oak rocker, her favorite. Let's see if it still has the same squeak."

Addie sat down and rocked slowly, smiling

and nodding as the familiar squeak began. She rubbed off a thin layer of dust as she felt the smoothness of the wood arms again.

"This was Gram's favorite rocking chair. She put her favorite chair in The Hideaway."

Addie wanted to look around carefully now. Gram had thought of everything. The stove was polished clean, the coal bucket beside it filled with charcoal. There were even sticks of kindling and a box of matches lying on top.

The bookcase near the door was nearly filled. Dad had been disappointed not to find the books he'd liked best as a child when he'd gone through Gram's things. Now Addie knew she'd find them on those shelves.

It was so like Gram to keep all this a secret — a surprise for Clay and her to discover by themselves. Or, after supper the first day, she might have said, "Addie, aren't you going to show Clay The Hideaway?" and then followed behind to watch their surprise.

Addie noticed something yellow hanging from a peg near the bookcase. It was Gram's old yellow raincoat—her slicker. She'd probably thrown it over her shoulders to protect herself against the early-morning dew in the woods and then forgotten it after a day's work in The Hideaway — maybe even the last day she'd been here.

Clay was opening the cupboards. He was excited, saying something about finding cans of food. But Addie barely heard him. She was fighting hard not to cry, yet tears were spilling down her cheeks.

She pulled the raincoat off the peg and stumbled out the door. She sat, then, on the steps of The Hideaway and buried her head in the smooth stiffness of Gram's coat.

She let the sobs come, not caring that Clay had followed her out. She could feel him patting her on the shoulder, but she didn't look up. She had not yet cried for Gram. She needed to now. She let the words come, all the painful ones...gone...forever...never again.

Once, when she'd sprained her ankle and was biting her lip at the pain that wouldn't quit, Gram had told her, "Don't fight it, Addie. Think about the pain, get to know it. If you can make friends with pain, it can't hurt you so."

Addie sat on the steps and cried, letting the hurt drain out of her. Clay kept patting her and saying, "It's all right, Addie. It's all right."

How long she cried, she did not know, but she was surprised at her stiffness when she stood again. The shadows had lengthened in the woods and the sunlight had dimmed. Without looking at her watch, Addie knew. They had stayed too long. They had missed the bus to Camp Witchetee.

She hadn't planned this, not at all. They would take another bus tomorrow, go on tomorrow, but tonight, tonight she — and Clay, too — would snuggle down in Gram's feather beds and sleep at The Hideaway.

Three

Addie pressed the phone so hard against her ear that it hurt. She was in the booth outside the Crossroads Grocery. A car had driven by, so she hadn't heard the man from camp clearly the first time. She'd have to hear what he'd said again.

The man's voice crackled with sleep or, perhaps, age, but there was no doubting the words when he spoke them once more. "I said I'll cross you both off this list 'n tell Miss Hankins you're not coming."

Click! The line was disconnected. Addie nodded into the receiver. He *had* said it! *The man had crossed them off the campers' list!* Was it possible? Could it really be that easy?

Addie turned her back to Clay. She knew he was watching her through the glass, but she couldn't talk yet. She'd been scared making

21

this long-distance call — her first on a pay phone—but she had had to call Camp Witchetee first thing that morning.

Sometime around dawn she had awakened with the thought that the counselors might be trying to contact Dad or the state police, or do something to find out why they hadn't arrived on the bus yesterday.

But that hadn't been so at all!

Tap! Tap! Clay was peeking in. He reminded her of a wounded rabbit she'd found once. The rabbit's eyes had been round and scared just like his. Clay thought something was *wrong*!

She pushed the door back. How was she going to tell him? She was bursting with words, but which should she say first?

"Clay, do you know what? There's been a mix-up. Camp Witchetee opens this weekend all right, but not Friday, not even today. We got started two days early! Imagine! They never even worried about us not getting there last night. They certainly don't expect us tonight. In fact ... " She leaned forward. How was she going to say it?

"The fact of the matter is they don't expect us at *all!*"

Clay pulled back. His lower lip was quivering. She'd have to talk fast.

"That man, the caretaker, or whoever he was, who answered the phone said none of the counselors were there. All gone to town for a last day of freedom, I guess. Anyway, when I told him our names and tried to explain why we hadn't come, he didn't understand. He thought I was telling him we weren't coming at all! There was a list of campers next to the phone and he crossed our names off before I could say anything. Can you believe it?"

Clay swallowed hard. He didn't understand.

"Clay." Addie grasped him by the shoulder. "Don't you see? We don't have to go to Camp Witchetee at all! They don't expect us. Isn't it perfect? Now we can stay. We can stay at The Hideaway, don't you see? We can stay all summer!"

It was out. What had been spiraling in her mind. Everything pointed to this. The man crossing them off the list had made her see it. Gram would have wanted them to stay. Dad would understand—he loved The Riffles.

"Addie, we can't, can we?" Clay's question was almost a whisper.

"Sure, why not?"

"I don't know. Won't Dad mind?"

"Oh, Clay." Addie began to pace back and forth in front of the phone booth. Her mind was clear; ideas were coming fast now. "Dad won't mind," she said. "He just wants us to be safe and happy. We'll be both safe *and* happy at The Hideaway."

She stopped, studying Clay's face as she asked, "You *do* want to stay, don't you? I mean really want to stay?"

"Sure I do. I've never been in such a great place before."

"All right," she said, and continued her pacing. "There's just letting Miss Hankins know officially. She's the head counselor. We don't want her getting upset. It's not enough to have us crossed off the list. Let's see. Dad's sent the deposit, but it was only twenty-five dollars. They said we would forfeit it if we cancelled at the last minute."

Addie stopped pacing to grab both Clay's hands.

"But that's all right," she said. "Twenty-five dollars is just a drop in the bucket compared to what we'll save him by staying here."

She released Clay with a parting shake and began to pace once more.

"I'll write a note, that's what. Dad says my handwriting is like Gram's, so it should pass without question. I'll say something like this: 'Adelaide and Clayton Scott Carver will be spending the summer elsewhere.' How about that? And then: 'I understand I am forfeiting the deposit because of this late cancellation.' "

Addie paused, then snapped her fingers. "And this, Clay, how about this?" She spoke the words slowly. " 'Would you please forward any mail that arrives for either of them to their Indianapolis address?' Perfect, isn't it? That's in case Mother writes to us. She won't be expecting us to be answering any questions — the mail always comes so crazy from Europe. We'll just get her letters when we get home. And Dad never writes. We are to call him after Sunday dinner, aren't we?"

Addie reached to touch the phone booth. "And, Clay, we *will* call him every Sunday. It's going to work. I just know it."

"Hey, Addie, you are going to tell Dad that we're staying here, aren't you?"

"Of course. Of course. We'll tell him — someday. But not right now. I know Dad better than you do. Telling him would worry him too much. You know how grown-ups are, don't you?"

"Yes, but Addie—"

"Clay, take my word for it. Dad'll just laugh when we tell him. You'll see. Just think, we'll be able to give Dad back all those money orders he made out to me. They are good for twenty years. They may even help us go to college. And we've got enough money—what with all that Dad gave us for any emergency for the trip and our whole summer's allowance. I even brought my birthday money."

"I did, too," Clay said. "But, Addie, how can we keep this a secret from the people around here?"

Addie looked at the store and her smile widened. It was perfect. Mrs. Groten never remembered her from one summer to the next. Just last summer, she had pointed a finger at Addie and had asked Gram, "Who's that?"

Gram had answered, "This is Adelaide, my granddaughter, who spends the summer with me."

Mrs. Groten had shaken her head. "No, your granddaughter's a little girl."

Gram and Addie had exchanged glances but hadn't said anything even though Addie had been almost as tall as Gram since she was ten. Gram had always been patient with Mrs. Groten.

"Just remember if Mrs. Groten seems a bit sullen or preoccupied sometimes, who she's married to," Gram had said.

Her husband, Honk Groten, was the only

person Addie had ever heard Gram call shift-less. Not for a moment did Addie think that he would remember her either. He always looked over the heads of kids as if they didn't exist.

Addie took a deep breath. "Clay," she said, "you and I are going into the store to stock up with supplies right now. We are going in just like two kids from The River Bend Campground. If I'm right, Mrs. Groten won't recognize me at all. If I'm wrong—well, I just can't be wrong, that's all."

Four

The screen door slammed behind them. They stood for a moment letting their eyes get used to the dimness. Little sunlight penetrated the unwashed windows. The only other light came from two 60-watt bulbs hanging from cords at opposite ends of the store and from a fluorescent light in the refrigeration case at the rear.

The Crossroads Grocery had been built as a gas station. Outside, the single pump, labeled GAS, and the air hose were the only indications of its original purpose.

Inside, it was different. Although it had been a store as long as Addie could remember, it looked so temporarily one. Remove the unpainted shelves lining the walls for canned goods, fold up the card tables serving as display counters and take up the piece of plywood over the grease pit, and, in less than an hour, it could be a gas station once more.

Something stirred behind the refrigeration case. A head rose and quickly disappeared again.

"It's Mrs. Groten," Addie whispered. "Come on, Clay. Help me load up."

Addie led the way to the shelves. There was a can of condensed milk and some soup left in the cupboard back at The Hideaway, but now she needed to think her way through breakfast, lunch and supper and get as many things as they could carry. A giddiness began to come over her as she filled Clay's arms and then her own. Each item was bringing them a step closer. Was she right about Mrs. Groten?

They couldn't see her behind the refrigeration case, but she must have been able to see them. As soon as they started for the table that served as a checkout counter, there was a shuffling. Mrs. Groten appeared and moved toward them, head down.

Although there was little gray in her hair, Mrs. Groten had always seemed old to Addie, and each year she seemed a little smaller. Her mouth was so fixed from years of not smiling that an arch had been carved above it. Without a word, she began the checkout.

Addie waited until she was almost through, then cleared her throat. "I'll... I'll need some milk, eggs and butter, please."

Mrs. Groten turned back to the refrigeration case without looking at them. Addie smiled and nodded to Clay. He knew she meant "I told you so."

Still, as Addie took out her wallet, her heart began to pound. Could it be heard? The store was so quiet. Her hand was shaking, too. Would Mrs. Groten notice her when she paid her? Was she waiting to say something then? The door of the refrigeration case slid closed. Mrs. Groten appeared again. But just as she did there was the clunk and squeak outside that could only be the halting of an old pickup truck. Mrs. Groten turned her head toward the faded curtains that hung in the doorway of the living quarters at the back of the store.

Honk Groten was Addie's least favorite person, but she was glad to hear him coming now. That noise had to be his truck. He was returning from his morning rounds of collecting pop bottles along the back roads at just the right moment to distract Mrs. Groten.

There was the sound of heavy footsteps, then voices — someone was with him — and then, that laugh, his laugh. Harold had become

Honk because of it. Addie had always thought it more like the braying of a donkey than the honking of geese, but Honk it had been since he was a boy. He seemed to like it. At least, he kept on laughing that way, punctuating almost every sentence with it. Once, when Addie was little, she remembered being scared into tears by Honk Groten and his big laugh.

The curtains split open and Honk Groten burst through, looking back, laughing at a sandy-haired man as tall as he but not as heavy.

"I tell you, Les, seventy-five bucks is just too much for a green hound."

Honk led the way to the pop cooler, fumbled around inside and came up with two grape sodas in one hand.

"You can't call him green, Honk. That dog has more sense about coons than any seven-year hound. I'm not kidding you."

That pleased Honk. Addie could see he was getting ready to laugh, pumping up, inhaling a bit at a time, managing to say in spurts, "I don't (snort)...think you're kidding (snort) ...about the dog..." He reared back then, his chest filling under the plaid shirt until Addie was sure the buttons would pop off before he exhaled. He did it all at once, smacking Les with a staggering blow on the back as he roared, "I just hope you're *kidding* about the seventy-five bucks."

Les pulled away. He shook the grape pop that had spilled on his hand down onto the floor and rubbed it out with his boot while waiting for Honk to stop.

"I'll let you try him out, Honk. You just see for yourself what a trailer he is."

Honk tipped the grape soda back. The drink disappeared as if it were being poured down a drain. Addie half expected to see him explode. The thought made her giggly. She busied herself helping Mrs. Groten sack up the groceries. Clay moved beside her. They only half heard the continuing conversation above the rustling of the sacks until Honk shouted, "That's just where we'll go! She'd never let me hunt there. Even in season, 'No hunting,' she'd say, but now..." Honk snorted again.

Mrs. Groten looked up. Les shook his head. "Well, I don't know..."

"Hey, Les, that place is crawling with raccoons. Why, I shot a big female there from the truck just the other morning."

"Yeah, but if Layne happened by..."

Layne was Fred Layne, the conservation officer for the county. Addie knew he'd been trying to catch Honk Groten for shooting out of season or on posted land for years. That's what Honk was really doing when he went out to collect pop bottles, Gram had said. He was taking potshots at anything that moved.

"Aw, Les. When did that ever stop us? Hey, you're not afraid, are you?" Honk reared back preparing for another burst of laughter. This time Les moved out of back-slapping range. "Afraid of ghosts, are you, Les?" Honk slapped his own knee.

Les shook his head while Honk rocked back and forth, laughing. Addie paid Mrs. Groten and without a word, picked up the groceries and marched from the store.

"They *are* talking about Gram! They are talking about The Riffles — hunting at The Riffles!"

She headed for the bridge without looking back. From somewhere behind her, she heard the screen door slam and knew Clay was following, but she didn't want him to see her face.

"What's wrong, Addie?" he'd ask; and there was plenty wrong! That Honk Groten! He could ruin everything, just everything! They couldn't have him prowling about or have any hound dog sniffing all over the place. The same man who would never go back into the wilderness would follow a hound trailing and not even realize it.

If only she could tell Fred Layne, but she couldn't tell anyone, not anyone. Angry tears filled her eyes.

It wasn't until she was halfway down The River Road that she was reminded of Clay again. She had been striding along, finding some satisfaction with the crunch her footsteps made in the gravel, when she became aware of an off beat — a skip, hop and shuffle behind her. Clay was hurrying to keep pace.

She took a deep breath and slowed down. Clay came up puffing, but a sideways glance told her it was from more than hurrying. His eyes were bright with excitement.

"Hey, Addie, couldn't we rig up something — a warning system in the woods to let us know if anyone's getting near The Hideaway?"

Addie stopped. She looked at Clay as if she'd never seen him before.

"Couldn't we?" he asked again.

Addie shook her head and said softly, "You didn't miss a thing, did you? You knew they were talking about The Riffles and Gram, didn't you?"

Clay nodded slightly as if he were afraid to admit it.

"Well, that beats all." Addie turned to walk on, slow now, so that Clay could stay beside her.

She *did* have someone. Funny, she'd never thought about Clay really being with her — he'd just been around her these past few months.

While she'd been sputtering mad, he'd been thinking up plans. What was it Gram used to say — "Plans are the tools for making dreams come true."

If they wanted to stay this summer in The Hideaway, they would have to make some careful plans. But why couldn't they? Weren't there two of them — two Carvers now to work it all out?

Addie shifted the bags of groceries to look down at Clay. He was smiling. She smiled, too. It was the beginning of summer, a bright day, and The Riffles was just ahead.

Five

Addie took her glass of lemonade outside. She would sit on the steps and watch the dark come.

It was the quiet time — that pause in the woodlands between the settling down of the daytime creatures and the stirring of the night ones. From beyond the woods came the sound of a car moving along The River Road.

What most people didn't realize (and no Carver went out of his way to tell) was that the high bank where The Hideaway stood was no more than the length of a city block straight through the woods from the Carver farmhouse. Addie wondered about the strangers living in Gram's house now. Would they be sitting on the porch like she and Gram used to after supper, nodding and waving to the evening drivers?

Gram hadn't seemed to mind, but Addie had

always resented it when others used the quiet little River Road as their own. There were only three farms on it, but it joined two county roads. On nice evenings, especially on weekends, it was a favorite "ride-in-the-country" route.

But Addie didn't mind it tonight. Sounds of the woodlands would soon blot out any man-made noise and, more important, Honk Groten and that Les with his hound would not risk coming to The Riffles on a busy weekend.

Her anger, her fear of Honk Groten ruining everything, had almost disappeared by the time they returned to The Hideaway. Not that they wouldn't have to be cautious. They were already saving tin cans to fill with pebbles as part of their warning system, but The Hideaway was a long ways from the meadow and looked so snug and safe that all Addie could think of was getting settled in.

They unpacked in the morning. After lunch they waded in the river to the sandbar and back and then spent the rest of the day making out schedules. Clay hadn't understood about that at first.

"Schedules? What for?"

Addie explained. "If it's written down, it's the *schedule* that says to do something, don't you see? It won't be *me* telling *you* to do it, or *you* telling *me* to do it. Gram always made schedules out for me."

Final copies now hung on the wall beside the sink.

DAILY SCHEDULE

7 A.M.	Wake up
7 to 7:15	Start fire and put on water
7:15 to 7:45	Wash and dress
7:45 to 8	Fix breakfast
8 to 8:15	Eat
8:15 to 8:45	Wash dishes, rinse with boiling water, air dry
8:45 to 9	Pick up clothes, make beds
9 to 10	Sweep, dust, bring in wood to dry for fire
10 to 11:30	Free time — write letters and read on rainy days, wade in river, etc., on nice days
11:30 to 12	Fix lunch
12 to 12:15	Eat
12:15 to 12:30	Rinse and stack dishes (save to wash with supper)
12:30 to 1	Rest and/or read
1 P.M.	Prepare for expedition of the day

Here's where Clay really surprised her. It was his idea to plan a daily expedition.

"Let's chart the woods, Addie. We can draw maps, put in the names of the trees, flowers and things. What do you think?"

Addie knew the woods by fallen trees, hollows and rises; and the river by bends, islands and sandbars; but she'd never drawn a map of it all. There were books on trees and flowers and wildlife in the bookcase. They really could identify a lot of what they saw. It added a scientific purpose that she liked to the summer, and it looked nice on the schedule, too.

1 to 4:30 P.M.	Expedition
4:30 to 5	Return to record day's events
5 to 5:30	Start fire for cooking and washing dishes
5:30 to 6	Fix supper
6 to 6:15	Eat
6:15 to 6:45	Wash dishes (lunch, too), scald, dry and put away
6:45 to 7	Bring in wood to dry for morning
7 to 9	Free time or do things on Weekly Schedule
9 to 9:15	Wash (including feet) and get ready for bed

9:15 to 10   Read and listen to radio for 10 minutes (to save batteries—only news and weather)

10   Lamp out

The Weekly Schedule was easier to plan. It hung next to the Daily Schedule with a blank sheet tacked under it for the grocery list. These were all things that needed to be done at least once a week, during free time as listed on the Daily Schedule.

WEEKLY SCHEDULE
Plan menus for the week
Go to store
Scrub floors
Wash windows
Collect wood and chop and stack under The Hideaway
Polish stove (at noon after it's cooled down)
Wash clothes

"How are we going to wash without a washing machine?" Clay had asked.

"Like the Indians and pioneers," Addie'd answered. "We'll do it by hand when it's needed. But we'll be in the river some part of each day. I don't imagine our jeans or shorts will need much more washing. We won't be wearing socks most times. As for the white things, we'll boil them on the stove. I've seen Gram do that. Then stretch them out to bleach in the sun."

She liked thinking they would be washing most of their clothes the way people had done it for hundreds of years. Addie leaned against the door to finish her lemonade. Clay was clattering around inside taking his turn with the dishes. She needed some time to think about him.

This had all happened so fast — in just a matter of hours. Clay seemed happy. Right now she could hear him humming to himself, but would he really like a whole summer at The Hideaway?

After all, he was a city boy, a *big*-city boy. Sure, he said he liked it. And it was true that last night he'd snuggled into bed without being told, and had looked up to tell her, "This is the most wonderful place in the whole world." But he was tired last night from the excitement of the bus trip. What about the nights to come?

Addie had always felt at home in the woods.

She remembered once when she was very small, she and Gram had been looking for wildflowers. All at once, Gram had stepped out of sight. Yet when Addie had realized that Gram was gone, she hadn't been afraid. The woods were all around her and she was simply a part of it.

It hadn't been that way, though, when Gram had disappeared behind the counter of the department store that same summer. Then Addie had been terrified. Although there had been people crowding around her, trying to comfort her, she had screamed with loneliness until Gram had come into sight again.

Still, Addie knew people who had lived near woods all their lives yet feared them, thinking they were a gloomy tangle of wilderness with snakes and sharp teeth waiting under every rock and behind every tree. Every rustle was a threat.

There were sounds, many sounds in the woodlands, especially noticeable at night. They were beginning now as the animals started moving about hunting for food and coming to the river to drink. The sounds were as normal in the woods as traffic noise in the city. But, what would Clay think of them? Would the woods become a dark and spooky place for him? At home, he sometimes awakened in the night. Dad had said it was because things were strange to him, everything different, but what about here...?

"All through," Clay's voice broke in. He came out and sat down beside her.

"It's getting dark," he said.

"It does every night, you know, Clay." Addie laughed, unnecessarily loud, she knew, but was he getting scared already?

"Clay, did you know if you wait for half an hour, your eyes become used to the dark and you can see almost as well as the night animals?"

"Really? Let's try."

Clay began turning slowly, first one way, then the other, his eyes widening as he searched the enclosing darkness. It seemed to Addie that as the light dimmed the volume was being turned up. Every buzz, flutter and snap was surely growing louder.

"Clay!" She was going to explain it all right now. "Just remember there is nothing in the woods that can hurt you. No matter what you hear. There's nothing to be afraid of."

"O.K., Addie," Clay said, continuing to turn his head from side to side.

"It's true. There's nothing that can hurt you in these woods. Of course, you've got to watch out for poison ivy, nettles, smartweed, things like that, but there are no bears, wolves or timber rattlers. In fact, there are no poisonous snakes of any kind at The Riffles."

"O.K., Addie."

"Not even snapping turtles or leeches in the river — the water's too fast."

"O.K."

"Why, it's been years since there have been badgers or wolverines in this part of Indiana."

"Boy, I didn't know about all those things," Clay said.

"Well, just forget about them. There's nothing out there."

"Except maybe skunks, huh?" he asked.

"Oh, sure. Skunks. But you don't have to be afraid of them."

"That's good," Clay said. "Look!"

He was pointing toward the back of The Hideaway where the underbrush had parted. His searching had not been in vain.

"It's a skunk, all right," Addie whispered. "But she won't bother us if we just sit still."

"Hey, Addie. There's more than one."

Clay was right. It was a parade of skunks. First came the mother, head up, tail up, marching forward. Four baby skunks followed in single file. The procession moved past the steps, close enough for Addie or Clay to have reached out and touched them. Yet not one of

the marchers so much as glanced at their ad-
miring bystanders.

Addie waited for the little family to disappear into the underbrush along the river's
edge. "I told you. There's nothing to be afraid
of."

"I like them," Clay said.

Addie nodded. "They are cute. Once I
picked up a baby skunk. Gram found the litter
in the machine shed."

"Did you really?"

"You know, even though I put that little
skunk right back where I found it, the mother
had moved the whole family by the next
morning. We couldn't find the nest again. She
made sure of that."

"She was a good mother, wasn't she?" Clay
asked.

"Yes, she was. In nature," Addie said, "if
there's only going to be one parent to raise the
young, it's almost always the mother."

"Sure not that way with people," Clay said.

"No, I guess people are a whole lot more
complicated. In the wild, the young have to
learn quickly to take care of themselves. The
mother gets them started, teaches them to get
their own food, protect themselves, find shelter—that kind of thing—and then out they go
on their own."

Clay stood up slowly, then moved on down to the ground.

"Do you think that's the way it is with Mother? Does she figure she got you started and now me, and it was all right to leave us?"

"I don't know, Clay. Gram said there were some things we wouldn't understand until we're grown up. But it might be." Addie wanted to change the subject.

"You know, Clay, if we don't bother that little skunk family, they'll probably come right past here every night. Skunks aren't afraid of anything in the woods. Even the fox moves out of their path. Those little babies are already big enough to squirt a fox in the eyes and blind him. Not forever, of course, but for a little while, and it hurts, too. A full-grown skunk can hit a target ten feet away."

"Did you like holding that little skunk?" Clay asked.

"Sure. It felt just like a kitten."

"Wish I could find one to keep," Clay said.

"You can't make a pet out of a wild thing, Clay."

Clay settled down again on the bottom step. "The only pet I've ever had that I could hold was a spotted newt," he said.

"A newt?" Addie asked. "What kind of a pet is that?"

"A friend gave him to me for my birthday. I called him Newton. I put him in the aquarium with my fish."

"But what can you do with a newt?"

"Watch him swim. He looked like a tiny diver. Best of all, I could lift him up in my hands and hold him above the water for a few seconds. Not long. I didn't want to scare him."

Addie had never thought much about pets. She couldn't have them at home because she and Dad were gone in the summer. And at Gram's there were always barn cats with kittens, a dog, baby ducks and chickens to cuddle whenever she wanted. But she had the most fun finding the nests and dens of the wild things.

Watching a litter of young woodchucks tussling outside their den or a goldfinch feeding a nest full of hatchlings was worth all the searching and waiting it took. She'd have to teach Clay what fun that could be. You didn't have to own something to love it.

But, she wouldn't tell him that now. She was finished talking. She just wanted to listen. For some time the frog chorus had been tuning up from the low place not far from The Hideaway. Now that night was here, it came forth full strength, a many-voice choir that easily drowned out the gurgling from The Riffles.

There was no moon. The sky above the river was filled with as many stars as the woodlands were with fireflies. It was difficult to tell one from the other. In fact, for that night the stars and fireflies might well have exchanged places.

Later, as the evening grew chilly, the chorus and lights dimmed. Addie and Clay moved silently inside and got ready for bed without lighting the lamp. They were just two more woodland creatures returning to their den for the night.

Six

Addie awoke in gray light. Clay was up, look-ing through the screen door. He was already dressed in jeans and sweat shirt.

"What time is it, anyway?" Addie asked as she reached for the clock on the floor beside the bed. Either the sun hadn't come up, or it was going to be an overcast day.

"Hey! It's not even five o'clock. We don't have to get up until seven."

Clay motioned for quiet. Addie stumbled sleepily to join him at the door.

"What's the matter?"

"Hear it?"

A shroud of mist floated over the river, pul-sating slowly up over the bank into the under-growth. There was a stillness in the wood-lands. Then from somewhere came a cry, a thin, sobbing cry.

"Yes. I hear it."

"I think something's in trouble out there," Clay whispered.

"I think you're right, Clay." Addie was fully awake now. "I'll hurry and get dressed."

She pulled jeans and sweat shirt over her pajamas and slipped into sneakers. Time was important. She was sure it was a distress signal, but of what?

Gram had once rescued two baby squirrels blown out of their nest during a storm. Their cry was a penetrating whistle. Gram had thought she was looking for a strange bird until she found the two huddled at the base of a tree.

"It could be anything, Clay. An animal, a bird, but something's wrong, terribly wrong. Come on."

Addie led the way through the underbrush. The mist was knee high. It parted, swirling away from their legs, then closed again behind them. They headed toward a rise, one of many that meandered like natural levees through the woods. Hickories, oaks and maples grew there.

They stopped to listen for a moment, but there were only the muttering peeps from a few awakening birds. No further cry came to direct them through the gray mist.

"Which way do we go now?" Clay whispered.

"Just wait. We'll have to hear it again."

Addie hugged her arms close. Even in the sweat shirt, she began to shiver. The woods were damp, chilly and so strangely quiet. Somehow Addie knew there would not be another cry. She waited, wondering how to explain it to Clay.

Then, as if a switch had been turned on, sunlight flashed through the trees. The mist faded quickly — a curtain rising as the bird chorus broke into song. The gray world dissolved into a golden one.

For the first time Addie noticed a large oak on the far side of another rise. Even from a distance, she could see a dark opening at the bottom. It was hollow — a good den tree.

"Come on, Clay. Quiet, now."

As they neared the place, Addie began searching the undergrowth. Clay moved ahead to circle the tree. He was behind it when he shouted.

"Here! Here! Hurry, Addie."

There was no mistaking what Clay was crouching beside. Between jutting roots of the big tree, lay a small female raccoon, on her back, her eyes closed. She was not much more than two months old, so young she had only

her fuzzy undercoat of gray, but the raccoon trademarks she was born with, the black mask across her eyes and rings around her tail, were easy to see.

"Is she dead?" Clay whispered.

Addie could see the tiny ribs moving.

"No, she's not dead yet. But, Clay, this little raccoon has nearly starved to death."

"We can help her. We can save her, can't we, Addie?"

"Now, Clay. I don't know what we can do. She's probably crawled out of her den in one of those holes up there, or maybe fallen."

"Please, Addie, we've got to do something. We can't just leave her here."

Addie shook her head and sighed. How could she tell Clay? This poor little creature was so near death she hadn't even opened her eyes while they were talking. What good would it do to take her back and let her die at The Hideaway?

"Addie?" Clay's eyes were brimful with tears, but his voice was steady as he answered her unspoken question. "Wouldn't it be better for her to die being taken care of in The Hideaway then out here all alone?"

"All right, Clay. All right. But don't count on anything."

Gently, Addie slid her fingers under the little body. She was shocked to feel the bones so close to the skin. She was almost afraid they would pierce through. As she stood up, she felt a shudder. Shiny button eyes snapped open.

"Addie! She's looking at us! That's a good sign, isn't it?"

Addie didn't answer. She held the raccoon in the palms of her hands as if she were holding eggshells.

Clay peeled off his sweat shirt ."Here, put this around her — keep her warm."

The mask that gives such a mischievous "robber" look to most raccons was curved downward giving this raccoon a sad, innocent expression. While Addie and Clay wrapped her carefully, she studied their faces. Then suddenly she did what babies have always done when they are frightened and hungry — she cried, rubbing her front paws, so much like tiny hands, into her eyes.

Nothing could have won Addie's and Clay's hearts so completely.

"Don't cry," said Addie.

"You'll be all right," said Clay.

"We'll take care of you."

Clay darted forward but turned back quickly to explain, "I'll go on to The Hideaway — I can find my way. I'll get a can of that condensed milk open, O.K.?"

"Yes. Do that, Clay. I'm not going to hurry too fast. I don't want to stumble with her."

"O.K." Clay started off again.

"Clay!" He stopped, clapping his arms over his bare chest and giving a hop-step from the cold and excitement. "Just don't count on anything," Addie went on. "She's in bad shape."

"I know, Addie. But she's alive."

He ran then, quickly disappearing behind the rise.

As Addie walked, she searched the little face for any change. The eyes stayed open, peeking at her from the folds of the shirt. At least she was no longer crying.

Addie wasn't going to get her hopes up, but maybe, just maybe, the warmth and jogging movement would keep life in the little body.

Seven

Clay had poured the milk into a bowl and stood holding it in the open door as Addie came up.

"Is she all right?"

"So far." Addie moved past him and eased herself into Gram's rocking chair. "She's too little, too weak to lap up milk from that bowl. Get me a clean dish towel."

Addie soaked a tip of the towel in the milk, then held it dripping to the raccoon's mouth, a tiny, thin black line that stayed firmly closed. Milk dribbled down making paths in the gray fur.

"She's not even going to open her mouth!" Clay sounded desperate.

"It'll take time, Clay. This is strange to her."

Addie dipped the towel again and again. The paths grew wider. The milk soaked through until Addie could feel its wet stickiness. Then, finally, two beads stayed on the raccoon's mouth. Perhaps they tickled or gave off enough familiar milky smell to coax the tiny red tongue out for a first taste.

There was a pause, as if the raccoon were thinking it over. Then, with a surprising show of strength, she reached for the towel, clamped onto it and began sucking out the milk.

"She's doing it. She's eating! I can see her swallowing!" Clay leaned forward to watch every movement, then reeled back to clap his hands.

Addie laughed as she tugged the towel loose and filled it again with milk. "She's doing it all right. But there's got to be a better way to feed her."

The raccoon's fur and Addie's clothes were becoming stiff with dried milk, but Addie kept at it. For nearly an hour she coaxed drop after drop into the little mouth. Then sucking stopped, the mouth clamped shut and the eyes closed. The movement was frighteningly quick, but the front paws kept wiggling, a signal that all was still right.

Clay whispered, "She's asleep, really asleep, isn't she?"

"Yes. She's exhausted."

"Addie, if she eats, she'll be O.K., won't she?"

"Clay, I don't want you to count on anything. I don't even know if we are feeding her right. The milk may be too rich or something. I don't have any idea how much she actually got into her. You can see most of it's on the outside."

Clay looked so crushed, she added quickly, "But she's alive. And look how peaceful she is now. That means something. Let's get her bedded down."

They laid the little raccoon, still wrapped snugly in Clay's shirt, at the foot of Addie's bed. Clay encircled her with pillows and then took up a vigil, standing beside the bed as if watching every breath would keep her breathing.

Addie hurried to wash up and change clothes. When she tiptoed back, she could see that the raccoon had not shifted her position;

not even her paws moved now, except to rise and fall with the breath of deep sleep. She looked so alone on the big bed.

"I'm afraid her mother must surely be dead," Addie whispered.

Clay nodded. "I thought so, too. That would be the only thing that would keep a mother raccoon from her young, wouldn't it?"

"I just hate to think what happened to the others," Addie said. "There's always more than one in a litter — even a first litter has at least two."

"You don't think they're still in the den, back in that tree, do you?" Clay asked.

Addie shook her head. "If they are, they're dead. This one must have been the strongest to crawl out, and we barely got to her."

"I guess, but still — "

"Now listen, Clay. I'm going to have to go to the store to get more milk. It'll be opened by now. Mrs. Groten always opens it — even on Sunday — by seven."

She said it as matter-of-factly as she could. There was no other way. She couldn't send Clay by himself, and they couldn't both go and leave the little raccoon all alone.

"I won't be gone more than a hour, maybe less. I'll really hurry. Just remember there's nothing in the woods that can hurt you. Clay, you won't mind staying by yourself, will you?"

"Me? No."

He didn't seem concerned. In fact, he hardly seemed to have heard her. Addie hesitated. Her sailor's cap was hanging on top of her Windbreaker. She plopped it on her head and gave Clay a snappy salute.

"Then I'll be shoving off, sir," she said.

Clay flashed a grin, but turned back to his vigil before she closed the door.

Eight

The sacks were heavy, two of them, loaded to the top. Even so, Addie jogged more than she walked. She could hardly wait to get back to tell Clay what had happened. Nothing bad, it had all been good from the time she'd walked across the bridge and seen that Honk's pickup truck had already gone.

If she had had to face him that morning, she wasn't at all sure she could have kept quiet. Hadn't he bragged about shooting a big female raccoon a few days ago? It just might have been the little raccoon's mother.

As she drew closer to the store, she recognized a car that made her turn and run back under the bridge to hide. It was Fred Layne's patrol car. She couldn't risk meeting him. He had stopped too often to talk with Gram not to remember her.

She liked Fred Layne. Once, he'd told her, "I used to hunt, but after two years on this job, I hung up my gun. You see too many animals hurt and left to die in the worst way to ever want to be the cause of it."

Addie tucked herself into the vee the bridge made with the sloping bank and waited for his car to leave. She didn't have to wait long. As it turned out, she was glad the incident with Fred Layne had happened.

It had made her think that perhaps she should be more careful about being recognized. Before leaving her hiding place, she stuffed her hair up into the sailor's cap and pulled the brim down so far that her face was half covered. No one would be able to identify her. Why, she might even be a boy.

How important this was she was soon to find out. Who would have thought that this would be the time Mrs. Groten would actually look at her, talk to her?

When she went into the store, Mrs. Groten

was sorting strawberries into boxes and kept at her work without so much as a glance in Addie's direction. Addie collected all the cans of condensed milk from the shelves. It took her three trips. As usual, Mrs. Groten seemed to know when she was finished and came forward, head down, to check her out.

Probably it was Addie's outburst when she spotted the baby bottles that did it. All she said was "Great!" but she did grab all six of them. And she supposed that all the baby bottles in the store and all the canned milk did seem a strange order.

Anyway, Mrs. Groten stopped checking, cocked her head and looked right at Addie (her eyes were surprisingly dark and shining) and asked, "What you feeding?"

It was a command to be obeyed.

Addie answered simply, "A raccoon. A baby raccoon."

Mrs. Groten nodded, moved to the shelves and came back with a bottle of corn syrup and a small brown bottle that Addie could see was cod-liver oil. Not until everything was packed into sacks did Mrs. Groten speak again. She chose her words sparingly, as if each one counted, and to Addie, as it turned out, they certainly did.

"Two parts water, one part milk sweetened

with a few drops of syrup five or six times a day. Cod-liver oil every day until it's weaned."

That was all. Mrs. Groten went back to her strawberries, and Addie picked up the sacks and went out the door without even saying "Thank you."

Mrs. Groten had actually given her a formula! The right way to feed an orphaned raccoon!

"We've really got a chance now. Maybe we can keep the little raccoon alive after all. Wait until I tell Clay!"

Addie couldn't hurry fast enough. Mrs. Groten, of all people. And to think she'd given the formula and *looked* at a person she'd never see in the store again? After all, Addie had been in disguise. It was just perfect!

But as Addie approached The Hideaway, she was suddenly fearful. The Hideaway looked so quiet. What if she walked in to find Clay crying because the little raccoon had died?

She could hear her own heart pounding as she climbed the steps, but there was no other sound as she hesitated outside the screen door.

"Clay?" She pushed the door open and stepped inside.

"Here," Clay said.

Addie nearly dropped the sacks at the sight

of him. He was standing next to the bed, his arms and stomach striped with scratches and scrapes, his face smeared with dirt. But he was smiling a wide grin.

"What? What...?" Addie started, then she looked at the bed behind him.

Two fuzzy heads were peeking over the barricade of pillows. Now there were two pairs of shiny black eyes looking at her from little robber's masks.

Nine

"I still can't believe what you did," Addie said, settling on the step beside Clay.

They had carried their lunches outside. It was past noon—almost time to call Dad—but it had taken that long to feed the baby raccoons the formula and get them settled. They were asleep now, arms around each other, tucked in the valley of pillows on Addie's bed.

"It never entered my mind that you were thinking about going back," Addie continued. "Through the woods by yourself. And climbing that tree! It's such a big one."

Clay nodded. "There was a vine growing up the trunk. I just grabbed it like a rope and went right up to the first branch."

"What if the vine had broken," Addie asked, "or it'd been poison ivy?"

"It didn't," Clay said. "And it might have been. Guess I'll know whether it was poison ivy when I start to itch."

Addie shook her head. "But reaching into that hole ... How did you know what was in there? Something might have bitten you."

"Nothing did. That little fellow just crawled right up my arm."

Addie shook her head again. "And I was so sure the others would be dead."

"I circled all parts of that den. Three times. I didn't touch a bit of fur. I know there weren't any others in there."

"Must have been a first litter then. From a young mother, too," Addie said. "But Clay, how did you know which hole in that tree was the right one?"

"It was the only one I could reach."

"Oh, Clay." Addie laughed.

"You know, Addie, I used to be pretty good at climbing the monkey bars at school and shinnying up ropes and poles in gym, but I'll tell you something—I've never, ever climbed a tree before."

Addie stopped eating and turned to study Clay. What a mess he was! His skin was streaked with scratches from the bark of the tree. A few, too, looked like they were from tiny claws. He should have put on a shirt, but she wouldn't say anything about that now. He had rescued the little male raccoon all by himself. That was enough.

"Seems to me, Clayton Scott Carver," Addie said, "that there have been several things you did today that you've never done before."

"Yeah." Clay's grin widened.

"Just wish I could tell Dad about it," Addie said.

"You can tell him we've found some really lovable new friends." Clay laughed, but Addie didn't join in.

All morning while they'd been tending to the raccoons, she'd been holding back, not letting herself admit that it was really happening. But there was no avoiding it. The little orphans were entirely their responsibility now. Addie and Clay were foster parents. It was up to them to raise the raccoons, to teach them to take care of themselves in the woodlands.

She counted on her fingers. At the most, they would be only five months old by the first of September, awfully young to be alone in the world.

But they *wouldn't* be alone! There would be two of them. If they were properly trained to find food and shelter and to defend themselves, they would have a good chance of making it through their first winter at The Riffles. Then by spring, if they wanted to go their separate ways, they'd be big enough to do it safely. Now, if she and Clay could only think like a mother raccoon...

"I've got a name for the little male," Clay said.

Addie looked at him sharply. "What did you say?"

"I thought I could name him and you could name the little female. What do you think of Prince?"

"Prince!"

"Yes. I thought about calling him King, but that's too big a name for such a little guy, don't you think?"

"Prince! For a raccoon?"

"Why not? I read a book about a dog named Prince. He was brave and strong and kind and smart and —"

"Now listen, Clay." Addie wagged a finger at him. "Those little raccoons in there are wild creatures, not puppies. We have them simply because they would die without us right now. We are *not* going to keep them and let them die later *because* of us."

"What do you mean?"

"I mean we are going to train them like a mother raccoon would. We're not making pets out of them. And don't you ever forget it."

Clay lowered his eyes, studying what was left of his sandwich.

"It's for their own sakes," Addie went on more gently. "We have to give them a chance to live in their world, Clay. It's the only place they'd be happy."

Clay finished his sandwich before asking, "We still got to give them names, don't we? We can't just call them He or She, or This One or That One, or Big One or Little One...Did you notice how much bigger the female is than Prince...uh...uh, I mean the male?"

Addie shook her head and sighed. "Go ahead. Call him Prince. Call him anything. But just remember what I said."

"I will, Addie. I'll remember."

Clay leaned back, cupping his hands to peek through the screen door. "They're still sleeping. Wasn't it funny how Prince put his paws up to hold the bottle just like a baby?"

"He was hungry," Addie said.

"I know, but couldn't you just see them both getting stronger with every swallow?"

"That's another thing," Addie snapped. "Those little raccoons may look like they are doing real well, but let me tell you, something

71

could happen — *bang* — just like that."

Addie didn't know why she had started this, but now that she had, she kept on.

"I remember a rabbit Gram and I rescued from a dog once. It seemed to be doing fine and then for no reason that we could see it died."

Not for one minute did Addie believe that this would happen to the raccoons. They were going to make it. They had the right formula now.

Addie ran her finger along a crack in the step, back and forth several times before continuing, "It's just that I've learned not to count on anything." She pointed her finger at Clay. "You'd better learn it, too."

"O.K., Addie." Clay scooted down to the bottom step. "But, Addie, nice things happen, too, that you don't count on." He turned to look back at her. "I mean, don't worry. We can do it. We can raise those little raccoons. Hey, anyway, what do you think you'll call the little female?"

"I don't know."

Addie stomped past him off the steps. Anger was sweeping through her and she didn't know why. Except that for just a second, Clay seemed to know something she didn't — as if he were the older one, being so understanding and all. But he didn't have any idea what they were getting in for — being responsible for two little lives.

Addie took a deep breath. "I don't know what I'm going to name her. But it *won't* be Princess!"

She picked up a rock, flinging it hard into the river. And then another, before turning back to Clay.

"You want to go with me to call Dad? He'll be expecting to hear from us. It's Sunday afternoon, you know."

Clay shook his head. "I'd better stay here. I mean, one of us should, don't you think? In case they wake up or something?"

Addie shrugged and started on without a good-bye. She wasn't going to worry about leaving Clay this time. He apparently felt safe enough in the woods. She would hurry, though. He certainly couldn't handle two wailing raccoons at feeding time by himself.

Ten

Names were important to Addie. People fit names or names fit people, she wasn't sure which, but a suitable name gave a source of strength that could always be tapped.

Just before Clay was born, Mother had been reading a book about a Southern officer, a hero in the Civil War. She had named Clay after him. Addie had been named after an Aunt Adelaide who'd lived one hundred years ago— a real pioneer woman. The stories about her were so full of humor and courage that Addie had been proud to have the same name.

When she was asked, "Adelaide? Is your name *really* Adelaide?" Addie would answer, "It most certainly is," firmly enough to discourage any further comment.

The name for the female raccoon would not

be carelessly chosen. It would fit a raccoon, but more important it would suit this particular raccoon.

Clay was full of suggestions. "How about Fearless?" he asked. "It took courage for her to get out of the den and down that big tree by herself."

"No, sounds too much like Shiftless or Thoughtless. It must be something grand. Intrepid! She was intrepid, wasn't she? Facing up to a grim situation, yet she didn't give up."

Then Addie looked at the little female raccoon sleeping with one leg flopped over Prince, her mouth open just enough for her tongue to slip out to one side.

"Maybe not quite so grand," Addie decided. "Intrepid really is more suitable for a battleship."

"You should name her Pounce," Clay suggested another time. "She's always pouncing on Prince and knocking him over."

The recovery of the starving raccoons had been remarkable. By the end of the first day, they were beginning to play with each other, wrestling, nipping and even growling a little. The female, being larger, did pounce more often.

"Pounce and Prince." Addie tried it and shook her head. "Too much alike. Besides" —

she leaned down to pick her up — "it won't be long before your Prince will outgrow this little girl and will be pouncing all over the place himself. Males are always bigger as adults."

"You ought to call her Cry Baby," Clay suggested disgruntledly when the little female raccoon awoke them at dawn.

Her cry of "*Waa Waa*" was as insistent and pitiful as a tiny human baby's. She seemed to have suffered the most from their mother's desertion and cried much quicker and more often than Prince.

This gave Addie the excuse to give her special attention. She was careful not to overfeed her, watching the clock and never giving her a bottle any sooner than three hours apart. To keep her from crying in between, Addie gave her water and carried her much of the first few days.

"I'm only doing this for now," she told Clay. "Just until we get her straightened out."

Clay didn't object. He began carrying Prince around, too. The little male quickly established himself on Clay's shoulder. He perched there unsteadily, clinging to Clay's head as if it were a tree trunk, while Clay moved about The Hideaway doing his chores. It became Prince's favorite spot.

Clay had surprised Addie while she was out calling Dad that first time by fixing a real home for the baby raccoons. He used a wooden box and a piece of the roll of chicken wire he discovered under The Hideaway. He nailed a plank over half the box and attached the wire over the rest.

"Clay, this is really great," Addie said when he presented it to her. She couldn't help but notice the unevenly spaced nails, some still sticking out dangerously. But they could be pounded in later. She was glad to able to praise him. She'd felt guilty about leaving so abruptly to phone Dad, but she felt good now. She had her own surprise for Clay, and then, too, the call to Dad had gone well.

"How do you like it there, Addie?" Dad had asked.

"We couldn't be happier, Dad."

"Clay, too?"

"He does nothing but grin."

"He likes the outdoors then? Not afraid at night, or anything?"

"Not a bit. He's becoming a real woodsman."

"They keeping you busy?"

"I'll say. We hardly turn over in our beds when it's time to get up."

"Well, I'm sure glad to hear that, Addie. It puts my mind at ease."

"Don't you worry about us, Dad. Not one bit." And then she ended with, "There's no place in all the world we'd rather be." Addie had hung up the phone flushed with happiness at how well everything was going.

"This'll be a good den box for the raccoons," Addie said after examining it carefully. "Deep enough and yet not too big. I didn't know you could build things."

"I didn't either." Clay grinned. "It isn't much really, but"—he leaned down to turn one of the bent nails—"see, it's like a latch. We can close them in the box to keep them safe whenever we are out of The Hideaway."

"And we're going to want to be out," Addie said, moving toward the door. "Come here. Look what I brought back."

Addie's surprise had been pulled up on the bank. Two tractor-size inner tubes.

"I found them in the pile of trash behind Groten's," she said. "I filled them with air at the pump. They haven't leaked yet, so I bet they aren't going to. What do you think?"

Clay hesitated.

"We can float down the river on them," Addie explained.

"Hey, that'll be fun," Clay said.

"It will be," Addie said, turning back toward the raccoons. Both were stirring again. "Whenever we have the time."

They had been so busy caring for the raccoons, splicing the most important things on the schedule in between naps, they had even put thoughts of the warning system aside, except for saving all the tin cans they were emptying. Vaguely, Addie's idea was to fill the cans with pebbles and string them together, spreading a web over the likely paths throughout the woods. Sound carried so easily along the river, she was sure they would hear anyone stumbling into them.

But two things happened on her next store trip to make her almost forget the danger of discovery by Honk Groten or anyone else. It had been only a week or so since she'd walked the river path, yet the path was already closed over with weeds. She'd forgotten how fast everything grew in June. Addie rolled up her jeans, stepped into the river and waded the rest of the way to the store. She was not going to trample down the barrier that nature was erecting for them.

Then at the store she heard Honk's voice coming from behind the curtains. He was talking, nearly shouting, into the phone.

"He's never patrolled up and down like this

except on weekends.... He's stopped every night to drink a bottle of pop, and then headed on down to The River Road just like he was looking for something.... Yeah, *two* some-ones, that's for sure," Honk snorted.

Addie had heard enough. Honk was talking about Fred Layne patroling past The Riffles. Layne must have heard rumors about Honk and Les's plans to try out the coonhound. She could hardly wait to get back to The Hideaway and tell Clay the good news.

"Snooper's what you should call her," Clay said when she returned. "I just sat and watched her wake up, climb out of the box and snoop all over this place. What she didn't poke her nose into, she poked her paws into.

Addie picked her up and let her nuzzle into the crook of her arm and up under her chin.

"No kidding, Addie. I don't think she missed a wrinkle in the bedcovers or a crack in the floor."

Addie scratched her behind the ears. "You're right, Clay. Curiosity is probably the most important characteristic of raccoons."

"*Determined* curiosity," Clay said. "You should have seen her work on the cupboard doors. She got them open, too."

"But I want her name to be something spe-

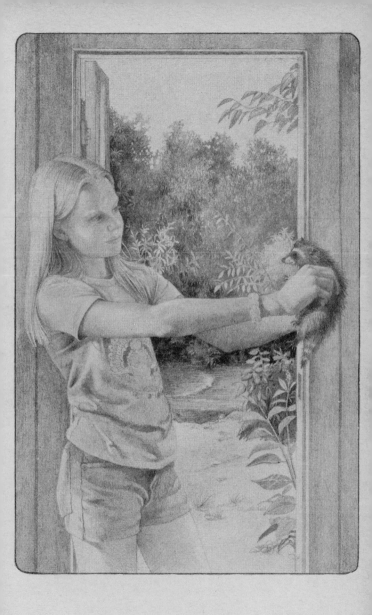

cial," Addie said. "Not cutesy pie. After all, someday she'll grow into a big mother raccoon."

Addie held her at arm's length with both hands. The raccoon curled around her hands like a woolly worm, but kept bright, steady eyes on Addie.

"She already has great dignity, don't you think?"

Clay didn't answer:

The female raccoon remained nameless until the following Sunday. Addie and Clay had had little chance to try out the inner tubes. For several days, the raccoons had had the routine of playing most of the morning and then taking a long nap after the noonday meal. Addie felt it would be safe to leave them sleeping, locked in their box while she and Clay floated down the river.

"We'll hide the tubes under the bridge," Addie said. "Then we'll go call Dad and buy ourselves a Popsicle at Groten's. Sounds good, doesn't it?"

It was a warm day, bright with sunshine and flickering shadows. The trip couldn't have been more peaceful. Silently, Addie and Clay let the inner tubes take them downriver, turning them gently around in the straight ways and spinning and bumping them over the riffles at each bend. It was fun, but neither Addie nor Clay allowed themselves to whoop or giggle. Without saying it, both knew as silent passengers they no more disturbed the fish below or the birds in the branches above than the pieces of sycamore bark and cotton-wood fluff that rode the river with them. They liked being a part of it all.

The return trip was different. Addie bought extra rope at the store to tie around the tubes so they could pull them back upriver. Now, squawks and flutters sounded from the wood-lands at their approach. It was impossible to wade quietly, so they joined the commotion caused by their splashing footsteps and laughed and talked all the way back to The Hideaway.

They were pulling the tubes up on the bank when they heard a high-pitched trill. Both rec-ognized it as a distress call and rushed to fling open the door. For a moment the call was forgotten. They stood, unmoving, astonished at the sight before them.

Boxes and pots and pans spewed from all but the highest cupboards. Covers and pillows tumbled from the beds. Books had been pulled from the bookcase and tossed onto the floor, a floor strewn with corn flakes, flour, charcoal and kindling. The last of a jar of honey was dripping from the counter, enlarging a puddle below.

There was no question who had done the damage. Prince was still in the box, clean and asleep, while floured footprints led from the honey puddle to a waving and wailing boot that had suddenly grown a small furry striped tail. It was the female who had somehow opened the box.

It was a time to either laugh or scold. Addie laughed and hurried on tiptoe through the mess, picking up boot and raccoon to quickly disentangle them.

The raccoon was a mess, glazed with honey, dusted with flour and sprinkled with corn flakes that now began to float like crispy snowflakes to the floor. With bright eyes, never more innocent, the raccoon looked at Addie without blinking and began muttering "*ub...ub...*," telling her all about it.

"I never saw such a mess," Clay said. "Bulldozer, Destroyer, Wrecker, that's what you should call her. Trouble's what she is. Just look at this!"

"All right. All right. We'll get it cleaned up, and her, too," Addie said. "She just opened a box she shouldn't have, that's all."

"I'll say."

"Clay, this little raccoon has just named

herself." Addie held her toward him. "Meet Pandora."

"Pandora?"

"Just like in the Greek myth," Addie said. "Pandora's curiosity got her in all kinds of trouble. Remember? She was told never to open the box, but she was curious and did. Then all the bad things — spite, hate, greed, that kind of thing — flew out into the world. But she closed the box again in time to keep one thing." Addie plucked off another corn flake and smoothed the raccoon's whiskers. "She kept *hope*. I like that."

"That's a good story," Clay said. "But, Addie, are you really going to name the little raccoon Pandora?"

"I most certainly am."

Clay made no further comment.

Eleven

Addie didn't say it out loud, but "things couldn't be going better."

The raccoons were thriving; Dad seemed happy with their phone calls — without the least hint of suspicion that they were not being made from Camp Witchetee — and she felt sure they were now safe from discovery.

Fred Layne seemed to have scared off Honk and Les. Besides that, the woods around them were closing in to hide them. Some of the weeds along the river were head high now and all of the leaves had grown full size. The canopy overhead was complete.

No longer did Addie run outside to check the wind before lighting a fire in the stove or adding fuel to it. She'd worried before that a column of smoke, especially on a calm day, would rise overhead like a finger to point at The Hideaway. Now the smoke had to filter through too many leaves to give anything away.

No longer did she wait until the curtains were drawn and the door closed before daring to light the lamp. She was confident no pinpoint of light could pierce the woodland screen.

It was summer, time for the first ripenings.

"Our expedition tomorrow afternoon," Addie announced, "will be to take the raccoons on their first exploration through the woods. Destination: the wild strawberry patch. It's near the road."

"Do you think the raccoons are ready for such a trip?" Clay asked.

"They'd be out exploring the entire woods by now if they were with their mother," Addie said. "I'm hoping tomorrow they'll start finding some food by themselves. I know, from the way the patch has looked after raccoons have gotten into it, that strawberries must be a favorite."

"But Addie, do you think that will be good for them?"

Clay had found a chapter in one of the books about a family raising a baby raccoon. Mrs.

Groten's formula was a little different from the one they used. They gave their raccoon vitamins, too, but the book did not mention codliver oil. Addie and Clay began to give the raccoons both to be safe. It did say that as raccoons' teeth come in — and Pandora and Prince were certainly getting all their baby teeth—they should have bits of lightly cooked vegetables, pieces of poultry, ground beef, dog food was good, and a little bit of fruit.

Addie had fixed them their first taste of solid food before Clay read the book. She thickened some of the formula with dry baby food, shaping it into a ball. This delighted the raccoons. They could play with it first, rolling it between the palms of their front paws, and then pop it into their mouths.

"It's just that the book said they aren't supposed to have too much fruit," Clay went on.

"Oh, Clay. I suppose that in the wilds the mother raccoon would say 'Not too much, you'll spoil your supper' when they came across a ripe blackberry bush or persimmon tree or something. Just remember, we've got to get these raccoons prepared to find all of their food by themselves before the summer's out."

Addie had bought dog collars and leashes for the raccoons. Pandora accepted hers unblinkingly and set out immediately, pulling Addie first one way and then another. No child turned loose in a toy shop could have been more eager.

Prince, however, clung to Clay's shoulder with three paws, and with the fourth pulled and yanked and twisted at the strange device clamped around his neck. When Clay put him on the ground, he rolled and rubbed trying to get the collar off.

"He doesn't like it," Clay said. "Can't I take it off, Addie? He'll stay with me. I can hardly walk two steps without him tagging after me."

Addie, led in a zigzag path by Pandora, had moved on to the brush behind The Hideaway. She called back, "If he gets scared by something and takes off into a tree, you may have to spend the day waiting for him to come down."

"I can climb trees," Clay answered, and bent down to remove the collar.

When he finished and started after Addie, he rolled his tongue, making a *"prrrt"* sound, and watched to see Prince's reaction. Clay had discovered the sound accidentally one day while giving Prince his bottle. The raccoon had stopped eating, stood up in Clay's lap, put his paws on either side of his face and then pulled Clay's head down so that he could look into his eyes. Clay was convinced he'd said something important in "raccoon." He was not surprised then to have Prince, happily free of his collar, follow him through the woods responding to his *"prrrt"* sound as well as a dog to a whistle.

Not until they had caught up with Pandora and Addie did Prince stop to examine anything. Pandora was sitting on her haunches, turning an acorn between her front paws. Prince watched until she dropped it, then pounced. Pandora snarled and pounced on Prince.

"Hey, you two," Addie scolded. "There are plenty of acorns in the woods."

The raccoons kept on tussling for a moment, and then as if a bell had rung, they stopped and started moving on together, noses to the ground, both muttering *"hm hm"* sounds of contentment.

Although the fuss was over, Addie filled her pockets with acorns to take back for playtime in The Hideaway.

The procession moved slowly now as the raccoons sniffed and prodded under leaf, branch and pebble and darted and lunged after butterfly and beetle. Anything that moved or was movable attracted their attention.

Pandora did not wait to get to the strawberry patch for her first taste of food in the wilds. She turned over a decaying branch, uncovering a mass of wiggling grubs. Before Addie could say "Yuk," Pandora had scooped up a handful and plopped them into her mouth.

The expedition couldn't have been better timed for ripe strawberries. The patch was a polka dot of red. As Addie had hoped, the raccoons didn't need to be taught to eat the strawberries. They plunged right through the patch, stuffing their mouths full until red juice trickled down their stomachs and dripped from their paws.

They were gluttons, yet dainty ones. Both pulled their lips back delicately as if afraid of soiling their whiskers, and then chewed each bite over and over. They paused regularly to lick themselves, especially to clean their fingers.

Before Clay could ask about it, Addie announced, "That's probably enough this first time." She coaxed Pandora into her arms with one last bite. "Come on, Clay. The expedition isn't over yet. We've got another stop to make."

"Not more ripe fruit somewhere?"

"No. We're going to Gram's house."

"Gram's house! You're kidding!"

"No, I'm not. I just want to take a peek at it. Show it to you."

"Will it be all right?"

"Sure, we'll stay hidden."

The raccoons were tired. Pandora cuddled in Addie's arms while Prince clung sleepily to Clay's shoulder. Soon they came to the rise that marked the old path from Gram's house to The Hideaway. It ran along the top of one of the natural levees that weaved through the woods. Addie called them levees because even in floods, water rarely went over them. Gram said she thought they were old riverbanks, much like the one The Hideaway perched on now. The undergrowth had not completely covered the path.

In a short while, Addie led the way up the slope next to the road and signaled Clay to keep quiet. She hesitated before pushing through the remaining thicket. There were no familiar sounds beyond the last branch. No clucking chickens, mooing cows, slamming screen doors. She'd never thought about the sounds before, but she missed them now.

Clay moved close behind her. She pushed the branch aside.

"Oh, Clay. Look!"

"I see it, Addie. It sure doesn't look like the house in the pictures, does it?"

"It's not." Addie's voice was flat.

Gram's pretty yellow house with white shutters had been painted gray—or was it aluminum siding?—and had black shutters now. The huge lilac bushes were gone. In their place were trimmed evergreen shrubs. Gram's old-fashioned garden, always a confetti of color with something ready to be picked, had been replaced with stately rows of untouchable red geramiums set in a bed of tiny white rocks.

"They've remodeled, haven't they?" Clay asked. He put his hand on Addie's arm just as she stiffened. "I'm sorry, Addie."

"No, it's not that. It's not the house."

It was easier, somehow, having strangers filling in the old places. The change had surprised her, that was all. What upset her was the fenced area near the garage. A dog was in it.

"Look, Clay." Addie pointed.

The dog was a coonhound. Its tail began wagging in a circle at the approach of a tall sandy-haired man.

"That's Les! That's Les going up to that dog." Addie felt like shouting it.

"Has he bought Gram's place?" Clay asked.

Addie nodded. Her voice was flat with despair. "Yes, Clay. And that dog is his prize coonhound."

Twelve

"I just knew things were going too well," Addie said, jabbing a hole into the side of another empty can.

To the delight of the raccoons, the floor of The Hideaway had become a network of tin cans and string. As Addie punched and Clay threaded, the raccoons pounced. Since returning from the expedition, Addie and Clay had worked steadily on the warning system, stopping only for a quick sandwich for supper and to feed the raccoons.

"Glad I picked up some acorns," Addie said. "It'll give us a start anyway."

"You aren't going to try putting this out tonight, are you?"

"Not all of it, of course. But I couldn't sleep if I didn't have something strung across that path."

"But, Addie, what do you expect to happen? That dog's penned up."

"Fine," Addie said, "but where will he go when he gets loose? The woods, that's where he'll go, and head straight for us. Don't forget a good hound can pick up a raccoon trail three days old."

Addie handed another can to Clay. "It's not just The Hideaway and us now," she said. "What would become of them?" She turned to look at Pandora and Prince. A minute ago they'd been playing; now, they were both peacefully asleep in a tangle of string and cans.

The warning system was completed the next day. Addie was pleased with it. String was now stretched across any openings that could be considered pathways. It was difficult to see in the daytime and would be invisible at night. The attached cans were easily hidden in shrubs and weeds, ready to rattle or spill out their contents if disturbed.

Checking the warning system became a part of the early-morning schedule. Sometimes the strings would be stretched by dew and have to be tightened, or the cans, if bumped by a passing animal, would have to be refilled. No such accidents were ever loud enough to cause a false alarm at The Hideaway. Addie wanted all strings kept about a foot high, so that small animals could walk under them.

"Any larger ones we'd like to know about," she said.

As the days went by without any disturbance, Addie began to relax once more and enjoy watching the raccoons develop in strength and skill.

They were fast becoming expert climbers. After supper Addie and Clay would sit on the steps while Pandora and Prince climbed the maple tree. Both were able to back down, but still needed practice coming off the tree head-first.

Addie felt it was important that they take raccoons inside before dark. The skunk family had continued to pass by The Hideaway each evening and she wasn't sure just how the raccoons would react to a meeting.

"If Pandora and Prince started getting fussy, those sweet-natured little pussycats might lose their tempers, stamp their feet and let the raccoons learn the hard way not to mess with skunks."

"I wouldn't want to be around for that lesson," Clay said.

"There'd be no living with them, that's for sure."

One evening Addie stayed out on the steps

after Clay had taken the raccoons in. The moon had risen above the trees, a white full moon. Addie had always been able to see a lady with flowing hair and long gown riding sidesaddle on an unseen horse in such a moon.

For a moment, she didn't believe that she'd heard the bark, but it came again, quickly changing into a throaty yelp, a yelp that could only be a hound dog moving fast, happy to be free in the woods.

There was more. A shout. A man's voice, then a whistle and more shouting. The prize hound was loose. Les was in the woods, trying to call him back.

Like a terrified animal, afraid the slightest twinge would give her away, Addie remained motionless, scarcely breathing. Then it came to her. She was sitting on the steps. The lamp was on behind her. Clay and the raccoons were inside — easy to trail, easy to see. They were going to be found, all of them, if she didn't do something at once!

Addie leaped to her feet and in one movement flung open the door. Clay stood wide-eyed with Prince on his shoulder. Pandora stood at his feet, one of his shoestrings dangling from her front paws. In that moment of shock, all eyes turned to Addie.

The den was threatened. Like a mother raccoon, it would be up to her to lead the enemy away, but first...

"Clay! The lamp. I'll get the windows." Somehow her voice sounded clear. Somehow, in spite of the sudden stiffness, her fingers worked the latches. The light was out. Darkness gave her courage. She knew the woods. The enemy did not.

"I'm going to lock you in. Stay quiet. No matter what happens, stay quiet."

"But, Addie..."

She didn't wait. The padlock was looped through the outside latch. Quickly, she closed the door and snapped the lock. She jumped off the steps and plunged into the brush behind The Hideaway at a full run. She leaped the ditch and started down the path, heading toward the barking.

She hardly noticed the clattering sound at her feet until she felt a slight pull across her legs. She'd run into the warning system. She broke the string quickly and slipped off the path, crouching down to listen.

The dog seemed to be zigzagging off in the woods to the right. She could hear Les shouting "Here, Blue. Come, boy." The only "coming" the dog was doing was coming closer to Addie. But maybe she could head him off, even hold him until Les got within range.

98

Addie hurried forward, listening for the barking. She hadn't gone far before rocks clattered around her once more. She'd run into the warning system again. As she stopped to break the string, a light flashed through the underbrush just ahead. More clattering, first to the right, then to the left. Les and the dog both had hit the strings.

"What is it? What's in here?" Les's voice was strained. He shouted, then, "Blue. You dog. Stop! Come on, hound. Let's get out of here."

But the dog continued to yelp. The moon was bright enough even among the trees for Addie to see him moving straight for her. She crouched low, her arms stretched out wide ready to grab him. Then, suddenly, not more than four yards away, the dog stopped. His yelping changed into demanding short barks. He'd found something and meant to stand his ground until his master came with further orders.

If he'd been any closer, Addie would have worried that he'd discovered her. As it was, she raised up slowly, hoping to be able to see what he'd found, but the brush was too thick.

Les stumbled forward. Addie could see the light flashing on his face and the tail of the dog, stiff now with excitement.

"What you got, Blue?"

There was a moment when no sound at all came from the dog, and only the faintest inhaling gasp from the man. Then both dog and man burst forth. It was a simultaneous yelp-shout. Addie jumped straight up in the air, but there was no danger of her giving herself away.

Dog and man had retreated through the woods at unbelievable speed, disappearing before the warm night air crossed the four yards to Addie to tell her exactly what the prize hound dog had found and shared with his master. There was no doubt they had met the skunk family. The smell was so pungent, Addie was sure that it had been all five skunks, and that all had found the meeting not to their liking.

She had left The Hideaway running in desperate fear. She returned stumbling in laughter.

Thirteen

The skunk affair was funny to Honk Groten, too. So funny that Addie began to feel sorry for Les. She told Clay about it while she unpacked the groceries the next day.

"You should have heard him, honking and snorting, making fun of Les. When Les drove up, Honk ran to the door and shouted, 'I knew you were coming five minutes ago. The wind told me.'

"That broke him up laughing. Then he held the door with one hand and his nose with the other and said, 'Why don't you just tell me what you want and I'll set it outside for you.'

"That started him off again. He sure thinks he's clever."

"It *is* kind of funny, Addie," Clay said.

"Do you know Les had to bury his clothes and stay up most of the night scrubbing himself and the dog? Let's see if I can remember what all he used — tomato juice, lye soap, kerosene, vanilla, and then finally, all of them mixed together. His wife still made him sleep in the garage."

"No kidding?"

"Honk teased him about the dog being ruined as a hunter."

"Will he?"

"No. He'll just stay clear of skunks. But Les's wife wants him to get rid of the dog for sure now. He's come down in price to fifty dollars.

"What'd Honk say?"

"Just honked some more. Les did say something that was funny, though. I'd sort of forgotten about all the running into the warning system. Les kind of joined in laughing with Honk for a while and then said, real seriously, 'Honk, there's something strange going on in that woods. I'm not kidding. There were noises like rattling chains first one place then another.'

"Honk burst out laughing. 'Ghosts, huh?' "

"Les chuckled a little, too, but then he said, 'No animal ever made such a noise. I'm not going back in that place.' "

"Addie, that's great!"

"Isn't it? Les is scared of us!"

Addie folded the sacks and put them away under the sink, then picked up a small bottle she'd bought and turned to show it to Clay.

"You know, Mrs. Groten suggested I use this instead of calamine lotion on my poison ivy. It worries me to have her take special notice. I wish there was some way we could get enough supplies at one time to not have to go to the store so often."

Clay didn't say anything until after lunch. Then he surprised Addie by asking, "What about the inner tubes?"

"What about them?"

"I mean," Clay went on, "putting something like chicken wire across them, making them into rafts."

"Clay! Clay, that's a great idea!"

"Well, I just thought the wire's bendable — strong, too — and we can pound the sharp edges into pieces of wood, so it won't poke holes, and then tie the whole thing on with rope."

"That's just what we'll do," Addie said. "I can haul enough supplies to last a week, I'll bet. Clay, you're beginning to sound like Dad, figuring things out like that."

It was the right thing to say to Clay. He made the wire rafts that afternoon and then surprised Addie by volunteering to go with her.

"If I go, too, we can take both rafts and get supplies for two weeks," he explained.

Addie couldn't believe it. As far as she knew Clay had never bought anything in a store by himself, but he was volunteering to do so now. She didn't say anything, but went ahead with plans to make the trip the following Sunday so they could call Dad at the same time.

The only problem was what to do with the raccoons. They couldn't risk leaving them in The Hideaway. There was no keeping them in the den box, and the mischief they could get into unattended could be disastrous.

"We'll just have to put their leashes on and take them with us," Addie said. "It'll be good for them to learn more about The Riffles."

"But what if they fall in the river?" Clay asked. "They can't swim yet."

"Oh, Clay, they'd swim instinctively."

Nevertheless, Clay tried coaxing them into deep water every chance he got for the next few days. Pandora and Prince would pace nervously on the bank, watching Clay, listening to his *"prrt"* call, but refusing to go beyond wading depth.

The Fourth of July was Saturday. Addie and Clay declared a holiday from all schedules to spend a day at the sandbar. While the raccoons played in the shallow water trying to catch minnows and crayfish, Addie and Clay held float races from the riffles at the bend nearest The Hideaway to the island in the middle of the river.

Clay, eyes closed, was just coming out of a spin after going over the riffles when Addie shouted, "Look! Clay, look!"

Prince was swimming toward him, head held high, ears back. Not far behind came Pandora, moving carefully through the water as if wishing she could swim without getting her fur wet.

Clay jumped up and headed toward shore. The swimmers made wide circles and followed after him. Addie and Clay shouted praises as the raccoons walked out of the water. The next moment the raccoons gave them a shower bath. Like dogs, Pandora and Prince shook themselves from head to toe as expertly as if they had done it all their lives.

Addie and Clay had to laugh at being caught so unawares. They built a fire to dry off and kept it going for hot dogs and marshmallows.

Pandora provided dinner entertainment by washing a marshmallow in the river. Both raccoons often rinsed pieces of food or favorite toys in water. The marshmallow, however, was far from waterproof, as Pandora was to find out—but not until it dissolved completely.

As raccoons usually do, she held the marshmallow under the water, turning and rubbing it between her front paws but never looking at it. Her paws might well have been detached from the rest of her body—doing the washing of the marshmallow entirely on their own—while she looked across the river, up into the trees and back at the campfire, unconcerned. When the marshmallow disappeared, she stopped short. While Addie and Clay rolled with laughter, Pandora studied her empty paws and then began searching the clouded water. Satisfied that it was gone, she licked off any remaining traces of sweetness and then bounded over to wrestle Prince as if the whole thing had been planned.

As evening came, nature provided the fireworks. Heat lightning flashed silently across the horizon — the perfect end to a Fourth of July celebration in the woodlands.

Fourteen

Addie muttered to herself as she hurried from the store. She should have noticed. All the signs of the approaching storm had been there: the heavy air—even Clay had asked about it— no dew on the grass, the birds so active, hurrying to feed as if there would be no more time to do it that day, and the raccoons acting so clingy. Most of the way downriver Pandora had held a near-stranglehold on her. Prince had clung to Clay without even fretting about wearing the collar and leash.

Yet she hadn't stopped to think even when Clay had made that remark about the raccoons acting so scared.

"Maybe they're afraid we're taking them someplace to leave them," he'd said.

What a thing to say! But she felt stupid that she had been so unaware of the weather. Any other year she would have noticed a drought. Not until now had she realized they had had no rainy days so far this summer—a few showers at night was all, but nothing to spoil their fun at The Riffles.

No wonder those farmers in the store had said they were glad to hear a storm was coming.

"Even hail can't get us all," one had said; "and there's got to be rain with that storm somewhere."

Addie searched the western sky. Was it already getting that yellowish color that comes before a bad storm? She couldn't see it well enough behind the trees to be certain, but the air was still now. It usually got that way just before a storm.

She shifted the sacks in her arms and looked up and down the road to make sure no one was coming before she disappeared down the slope and under the bridge. Clay was already on his feet, holding the leashes out to her.

"I'll hurry" was all he said as he brushed by. She hadn't really seen his face, but she was sure he'd be all right. She'd caught him practicing reading his list behind The Hideaway that morning.

It didn't occur to Addie not to have Clay go to the store, even with a storm approaching. His list was shorter than hers, and besides, Dad had said when she called him that he'd be gone next Sunday. That meant with the supplies they were getting now there would be no reason to leave The Riffles for two weeks.

Pandora and Prince clamored to be picked up, but she couldn't stop now. She looped their leashes over a sapling. She'd have to work fast getting the rafts ready. The raccoons could help her most by keeping out of the way.

Quickly, Addie unpacked the sacks and re-packed everything in large plastic bags, spreading the weight evenly on the rafts. One bag, she decided, was loaded enough to be closed up and tied securely with the ropes. The other she left open for Clay's things.

As she finished, she heard the first rumble of thunder in the distance. Pandora and Prince had been pacing and fretting; now both strained upright on their leashes, pleading with Addie.

"It's all right," she said, scooping them up. They wiggled and pushed into her arms, trying to find a place to bury their heads and escape the thunder.

Addie didn't blame them. She remembered the night thunderstorms when she was little—

how she would pull the covers over her head no matter how hot it was, arranging a small tunnel for her nose, and plugging her ears with her fingers.

Pandora and Prince couldn't do all that. If they had been in the woods with their mother, they'd all be huddled together in their den by now.

"I got everything," Clay said.

Addie turned quickly. She hadn't heard him coming. His face was flushed.

"I didn't forget a thing. Mrs. Groten didn't even look at me. All they were talking about was the weather. Did you know a storm's coming?"

"Yes," Addie said. "You take the raccoons and let me get the other raft fixed."

As soon as she finished, she tied another length of rope to opposite sides of each of the rafts, making large loops to serve as simple harnesses. Addie slipped the rope of one raft over her head and positioned it at her waist. Then she maneuvered the other raft over to Clay.

"Give me Pandora," she said, holding the rope out to him. "And get this around your waist like I did. We've got to hurry."

The temperature had already begun to drop. The leaves in the sycamores across the river were twisting in the first breeze of the approaching storm.

They had not expected pulling the loaded rafts to be easy. The round tubes were not shaped to cut smoothly through the water. However, the current was slower than it had ever been and the water glass clear. They made good time.

As they neared the first bend, a school of baby catfish zigzagged past them, heading for the shadows of overhanging grass along the bank. They were soft black with tiny whiskers, miniatures of the fierce-looking adults they would become. Any other time Addie would have called a halt to watch them, but now she hurried on.

As she led the way around the bend, the wind that had been skirting the treetops swept across the meadow and caught her full force. She staggered sideways.

"Are you all right?" Clay shouted, but he was hopping, too, trying to keep his balance.

Addie nodded and grabbed a tighter hold on Pandora and the rope around her waist. For the first time they could see the line of black that stretched across the western horizon. Roiling clouds were moving swiftly, reaching to blot out the sun that still shone overhead.

"It's really going to storm, isn't it?" Clay had

moved up beside her, his eyes nearly closed against the wind. He held the rope with one hand and a bulge in his shirt with the other. Prince had taken refuge inside. "What are we going to do?" he asked.

"Keep going, Clay. As fast as we can."

The wind rippled the water and tugged sideways at the rafts. They could no longer see where they were stepping and both began stumbling over the rocks. Pandora grew more restless. Addie leaned over her, trying to shield her, holding her even tighter as the thunder rolled closer, crashing louder and more often now. It was step, stumble, step again.

Just when Addie felt they weren't moving at all, the water deepened. They were rounding the next bend, heading into the woods. The sandbar would be the next turn, then one more and The Hideaway.

Smack! The wind gusted as they changed direction. It pushed the raft hard into Addie. So hard, she dropped Pandora and fell head-long into the river. Both came up sputtering. Pandora started swimming for shore. Clay plunged after her, managing to grab her leash just as she scrambled up the bank.

Addie splashed up to Clay, dripping wet. "Give me your raft." She knew this was what needed to be done and began pulling the rope over Clay's head. "Take the raccoons back to The Hideaway. Hurry. You can beat the storm through the woods. Just hurry!"

Clay started to protest, but the wind was with them now and the rafts were already pulling Addie on upriver. She made such good time that as she passed the sandbar, she began to hope that maybe she, too, could make it back to The Hideaway before the storm broke.

But as she rounded the island, the first drops of rain hit the water in front of her. She was too wet to feel them, but she saw them, falling slowly, big drops, making deep pits.

There was a crash of thunder, so close Addie jumped in spite of herself. The rain came then, churning the water around her. The wind grabbed the rafts, spinning them, first in front of her, then behind her. Tree branches whipped like rope overhead.

Addie stumbled on blindly now, not even noticing when she bumped against the big rock at the last bend, scraping her leg. The pain would come later.

Another crack of thunder. A tree branch split and fell behind her, just missing the rafts. Addie heard a scream. It had come from her. She'd never been afraid in the woodlands before, but this was a world gone mad.

A blur of color moved along the bank. It was coming toward her.

"Clay!" she shouted, knowing her voice was lost in the wind, but certain it *was* Clay. He'd left The Hideaway to come help her.

Together, they pulled the rafts the rest of the way. They carried them, sacks and all, first one and then the other, up the bank and into The Hideaway, slamming the door on the storm at last.

Addie and Clay stood breathless, blinking water out of their eyes. The raccoons, across the room, became clear to them at the same time. If Addie had been worried about Pandora and Prince knowing how to defend themselves, all doubt was erased at that moment.

The two stood ready to repel the invasion of the dripping monsters. They had taken the fighting stance used by their ancestors. Their backs were arched high, their noses almost touching the floor. They were protecting their soft undersides, yet they stood with forelegs spread wide, ready to spring in attack. They growled, curling their lips back. They may have been fuzzy and still losing their baby teeth, but surely no pair of three-month-old raccoons had ever looked more fierce.

"They don't know us," Clay said.

"No wonder." Addie started to giggle. She

had to look at least as bedraggled as Clay and he looked like a rat thrown up on the beach. Laughter bubbled out of her uncontrollably. She did manage to say, "You look awful."

Clay bowed from the waist, a dripping courtier. "Same to you, Madam," then burst into laughter, too.

They pointed to each other, then to the raccoons and back again, laughing together until they sank to the floor in joyous relief at being safe in The Hideaway once more.

Fifteen

The rain didn't stop with the storm, but continued the next day and then the next and the next until the ground became saturated and the river began to rise, and still it rained.

"Is it going to flood?" Clay asked. It was the fourth time in a half hour that he'd looked out the windows and then the door.

A stream was developing in the ditch behind The Hideaway. In front, water had risen more than halfway up the bank. The lower bank on the other side of the river was already under water. The riffles at the bend had long since disappeared and only a swirl marked the big boulder in the middle of the river.

"It *is* flooding," Addie answered, shrugging her shoulders. "Once it's out of its bank, anywhere, it's a flood. Don't worry, Clay. This high bank has never been under water."

"I don't know, Addie, I'm not much of a swimmer."

"Oh, Clay. No one's going to have to swim."

Still, Addie began slipping to the door and looking out the windows herself. The rising river hadn't bothered her before. In fact, she'd found it especially cozy in The Hideaway these rainy days.

There were no gutters on the roof, and rain streamed past the windows in moving sheets. Addie liked the feeling that they were hidden, warm and dry, behind a waterfall. They had started a fire in the stove that first night to dry off, and kept it going just enough to keep out the dampness.

All thoughts of schedules, even the rainy-day items, had been put aside. There was no chance of being on a schedule while confined with two raccoons. No longer did they move about unsurely. Now it was bound and jump and climb — definitely climb — up the chairs, up the cupboards, up the curtains and sometimes up Addie's or Clay's legs.

Keeping them safe and out of mischief was a full-time job. Fortunately they continued to take naps at the same time, retreating to their box to snuggle together while Addie and Clay put things in order once more.

The raccoons were still asleep as Clay turned from the door again.

"I can't remember what the sun looks like."

Addie was drying clothes on lines strung across The Hideaway. Towels and rags had to be positioned directly under each piece to catch the drips. She stopped her work.

"Clay, poke up the fire. What we need today is Gram's vegetable soup. We'll put it on the stove and let it simmer until we get so hungry smelling it, we'll have to stop and eat it."

Addie pumped water into their biggest kettle, added beef bouillon cubes, and then peeled and sliced carrots, celery, onions and potatoes.

"You make it with any kind of vegetables on hand," she explained. "I'll add canned green beans and maybe corn before we eat it. Open the tomato juice, too, Clay. That, with a pinch of sugar, really is the secret."

"Sugar?"

"Gram always added sugar to anything that had tomatoes in it. She even put sugar on sliced tomatoes instead of salt."

"Bet that still wouldn't make the raccoons like them," Clay said.

Pandora and Prince, they'd discovered,

would try anything from cooked cabbage to red soda pop, anything, except tomatoes.

"Well, the early pioneers wouldn't eat them either, you know," Addie said. "They thought they were poisonous."

"Maybe they are to raccoons," Clay said.

The rest of the day, The Hideaway was filled with the tangy aroma of the simmering soup. Addie propped up pillows on the floor and worked on the record book. The black-eyed Susans were in full bloom in the meadow. The red-winged blackbirds and grackles, with nesting season over, were already gathering in flocks to feed along the river, a reminder that although summer was in its prime, it was moving on.

When the raccoons awoke and began removing every book from the bookcase and then taking off all the covers, Addie didn't stop them. They weren't tearing the books and it kept them busy and content. Maybe Clay'd been right when he'd teased her about how she was changing—"easing up" was the way he'd put it.

Clay certainly wasn't easing up about the rising water. He couldn't settle down with a book. Besides checking the windows and door, he began turning on the radio to hear the weather report of "continued showers."

"Don't worry so," Addie said. "It'll stop before they predict it. And no matter, we've got plenty of food, plenty of firewood. We're perfectly safe."

"Sure hope you're right," Clay said.

"Aren't I always?" Addie laughed.

It wasn't doing any good to worry, she thought. The best thing was to keep busy. When she went to bed that night, she concentrated on plans to cook chocolate pudding the next day, and tried to forget the patter of the rain continuing on the roof.

She was nudged awake by a cold touch on her cheek — Pandora's nose.

"Hey, none of this," Addie said. It was light outside, but early. Addie tucked Pandora under her arm and shoved the covers aside. "It's not time to get up, and you're not sleeping with me."

Pandora twisted, nuzzling so hard to bury her head that Addie almost dropped her.

"What's the matter with you?"

Clay popped up from the trundle to answer. "Nothing."

Addie started to laugh but caught her breath instead. What was that sound? It was outside, a rushing wind sound, yet nothing like wind was tugging at The Hideaway.

"Clay!" she gasped, but he'd heard it, too, and was already running to the windows.

Addie hugged Pandora tightly. She could feel the raccoon's heart pounding, but no faster than her own at the sight before them.

Dead tree branches, uprooted brush swept by, rolling over, going under and then popping up again in the distance. Sometime during the night the overflowing river had turned into a swirling, churning flood.

Clay ran to fling open the door.

"It's the same here."

The Hideaway and the two maples on either side of it now stood alone on a hump of land. They were on a tiny island with a brown and foaming shoreline. The other trees stood in running water with brush waving like sea-weed around them.

"Addie, what are we going to do?"

She'd almost forgotten Clay's on-the-brink-of-tears look, but then she didn't blame him. Only once before had she seen the river like this. She had been with Gram at the meadow. She'd trembled watching it, but then it had been rushing by in front of them. That was far different from being on a circle of ground with the flood sweeping around you on all sides.

"What can we do?" Clay's face was white.

She had to think of something, but her mind was a blank. All that came to her was a silly verse she and Gram had laughed over:

> *When in danger,*
> *Or in doubt*
> *Run in circles,*
> *Scream and shout.*

They'd been sitting at the kitchen table when Gram had said it. What else was it she'd said?

"There's nothing wrong with being scared. What's wrong is not *doing* anything about it. Face it. Face the danger. The tiger you're cowering from will turn into a kitten."

That was it! Addie put Pandora down. "Clay, come on."

She led the way outside to stand on the steps. Clay followed automatically kicking back to keep the raccoons from slipping out, too.

"Look, Clay! We aren't the only island."

Water in the ditch behind The Hideaway swirled almost as fiercely as in the main channel, but it was not more than ten feet wide, and just across it was the finger of land, the old path through the woods to Gram's. They could see it twisting through the water, a walkway to the higher ground near the road.

"Let's make this tiger into a kitten," Addie said.

"What?"

"Never mind, Clay. All we have to do is figure out how to get over there."

"Hey, Addie." Clay grabbed her arm. "I can't swim that well. And what about the raccoons?"

"Swim! Listen, Clay, the strongest swimmer in the world would be a nut to go into floodwater. It's a whirlpool, even where it isn't deep. It can pull you under."

"But, how...?"

"That's just it. We've got to figure how."

Addie moved off the steps to look under The Hideaway.

"Maybe there's something under here we can use to build a bridge of some kind...."

"No," Clay said. He was looking up into the trees. "Not a bridge, Addie, a swing."

He pointed to the maple. "We've got plenty of rope. We can tie it to that branch up there. Stand on that low one and swing across just like Tarzan."

Addie put her hands on her hips and looked up, down and across. She jumped back up on the steps. The bear hug she gave Clay surprised him.

"Clay! You're just something!" Seeing the flush spread over his face, she patted him on the back instead of giving him another such hug, although she felt like it. "That's exactly what we'll do. It's a perfect answer."

"Well, if you think it's all right . . . I mean we have plenty of rope and all. . . ."

"All right! It's great! But then I guess I shouldn't be surprised that the son of an engineer could figure things out."

"Yeah," Clay said. "That's right." He turned to lead the way into The Hideaway.

Sixteen

Something was bothering Clay. Six weeks ago Addie might not have noticed, but she knew him now well enough to know it was more than just being quiet.

She'd asked him if he'd hurt himself — climbing the tree or swinging or jumping — but he'd just shaken his head. He'd stayed in this strange mood all day, not changing even when the rain stopped and the sun burst out in a sky so clear there was no doubt the rain had ended for good.

"You just watch," Addie had said. "This water will start going down now as if a plug had been pulled."

He'd nodded, but said nothing.

Even when she'd asked outright, "Clay, just what *is* the matter?"

He'd answered, "Nothing."

Addie couldn't figure it out. The day had gone well as far as she could remember.

Clay had worked happily, playfully fighting off the raccoons as he held the clothesline rope for her to braid. They'd decided they needed the extra strength of braided rope for their swing.

He'd seemed genuinely pleased when Addie agreed that his lighter weight made him the best choice to take the rope out on the big branch they'd chosen to tie it to. In fact, he'd been a bit cocky about it.

"It'll be a cinch," he said. "Try coming down a tree trunk holding a baby racoon and expecting the vine you're clinging to to break off any second. Now *that's* scary."

He'd readily agreed that Addie as stronger swimmer (just in case) should be the first Tarzan. Everything worked as they'd planned it.

They tied the garbage-can lid onto the end of the rope as a place to sit or stand and then attached two other lengths of rope to it. Addie slipped one of these ropes around her wrist, Clay held the other. This way at least one of them would always have a hold on the swing. There would be no danger of losing it, letting it get away from them to dangle midstream and out of reach.

Addie pushed off and swung back and forth three times, then, yelling "Wahoo," dropped onto the opposite side of the ditch. She held the garbage-can lid over her head in triumph and shouted back to Clay, "We did it! It's great!"

She swung back quickly to let Clay take his turn. "It's perfectly safe, Clay. Just don't think about the water. You're just going for a swing, that's all."

"I hope not a *swim*," Clay said.

But he did fine. He pushed off, did his imitation of the Tarzan yell and swung over, jumping off the first time in a wide arc. He laughed as he sprawled forward on all fours in the mud, but got up quickly to wave to Addie. He'd seemed perfectly all right.

Clay didn't get back on the swing right away, but walked along the path. He knelt down and then stood up again to look through the trees toward the road. Addie shouted to him to hurry back.

The swing was going to work fine — for escape, if need be, and certainly for fun. She was ready to settle in and get started cooking the chocolate pudding.

Clay had come back and the quietness set in. Addie didn't think much about it at the time, but became concerned as the day went on.

Clay kept going to the door, even after the rain stopped, no matter how much she reassured him about the water going down. They were so close to the headwaters of the river, floods always drained away quickly.

As tired as she was, she wasn't going to be able to sleep if she didn't find out just what was bothering Clay.

The raccoons were having what Addie was counting on as their last romp that day. It was still light, but she had fixed an early supper, hoping that everyone would go to bed early. It had been a long day.

She dished out the rest of the pudding, gave a bowl to Clay, who was sitting cross-legged on his trundle bed, and took hers to the rocking chair to eat.

"You know, Clay," she said, licking the pudding from the spoon slowly, "we've figured out lots of things together this summer. Become kind of a team, wouldn't you say?"

Clay continued eating, but she knew he was listening.

"I guess I never thought before that a brother and sister could do anything other than fight," she went on. "Frankly, I was happy the way things were before you came. I liked being the only one with Dad at home, and Gram in the summer. I didn't see much sense in your coming to tag along.

"But, you know what?" Addie looked at Clay's bowed head. He was busy scraping the last of the pudding. "I don't feel that way now. In fact, I think it's pretty great having a brother to stand beside you, no matter what the trouble is, you know, someone to share good things and bad things with."

Clay got up and took his dish to the sink. Prince grabbed him around the leg. He picked Prince up and set him on his shoulder before turning to face Addie.

"O.K. There's no easy way to tell it. But it's still light enough for you to see for yourself, Addie. Take the swing over and look at the path."

Numbness came over Addie as she knelt to examine the ground on the other side of the ditch. It hadn't been hard to find what had been bothering Clay. *Boot tracks*. The light rain that morning had not erased the ridges.

Addie looked back at The Hideaway. No one could have stood at this place without seeing the smoke coming out of the chimney, even the muddy shoes outside the door.

"Whoever made those tracks knows The

Hideaway's being lived in," Addie told Clay when she returned. It was a statement of weary despair.

"But I don't think they know it's us," Clay said. "That's what I've been fretting about all day. If someone thought something was wrong — we were runaways, tramps or something like that — we'd have heard from the sheriff or Fred Layne by now. But no one's come and it's almost dark. I think we're all right."

Addie shook her head slowly, her voice still flat. "What did the tracks look like to you?"

"Oh, boot tracks. Not too big. Must have been a small man."

"Or," Addie said, "a big man with little feet. Well, it won't do any good to worry about it tonight. Let's get some sleep."

Addie wanted to get to bed so she could think. She locked the door and turned off the lamp and spent the most restless night she'd had since coming to The Hideaway. Along toward morning, Pandora crawled out of the den box and slipped up to lie down on Addie's pillow. This time she was allowed to stay.

Seventeen

Addie had faced hunters, storm and flood, but nothing like the footprints. She couldn't get the picture out of her mind. Someone had walked along the path in the early morning, or perhaps late at night. Someone had stood over there and looked at The Hideaway. If it had been at night, the lamp would have been on— they'd been leaving it on low — and in the daylight the signs of The Hideaway being lived in would have been just as obvious. Someone knew their secret.

Clay became convinced it had been mere chance.

"Someone parked along the road and followed the high ground back to see the flood," he said. "They just thought The Hideaway was another summer place. Since we weren't in danger—so close to the high ground and all—nothing more came of it."

That was Clay's explanation. He'd been so upset about it that first day, and now he was ready to forget it. As the river went down, his spirits soared. He began outlining the shore of their island with sticks. Each time he moved them back, he ran to Addie with a report.

"We'll be out of the woods, or"—he laughed—"I mean, *back* in the woods, real soon. You were right, Addie. The plug's been pulled. This flood's going down the drain."

Addie couldn't join in his cheerfulness. She had never felt so exposed. Most of the weeds had been too dry to withstand the rushing waters. The woodland barricade had been pushed down or carried away.

Addie couldn't keep from going to the door and looking across the ditch. Yet each time she did, she dreaded that she might actually see someone standing there.

She continued to let Pandora sleep with her and began picking her up and holding her almost as much as she had the first week. Only this time it was for her sake, not Pandora's; and the raccoon usually wiggled out of her arms after a few moments—impatient to get going again.

When Clay commented on it, Addie answered, "Mother raccoons are very loving with their children. They discipline them, train them *and* cuddle them."

She didn't say anything more about it, but she knew Clay was wondering why, when she had been so insistent that they not treat the raccoons as pets, she was treating Pandora so much like one now.

She wasn't sure herself, except that after all these weeks together, she couldn't stand the thought of something happening to spoil it. And, what would become of the raccoons if they were discovered now? They were still too young, not more than four months old at the most. They couldn't be turned loose at The Riffles yet.

Even if the impossible happened, and Dad let them make a place for the raccoons at the duplex, it couldn't last for long. Prince and Pandora wouldn't be happy unless they could explore the world freely. That's what she'd always wanted for them.

And there was little guarantee that they wouldn't become fierce, or at least untrustworthy, as they matured. After all, they *were* wild creatures. Addie and Clay had already been nipped hard enough to hurt.

She'd seen what happened to raccoons who

had become pets as playful babies and then had grown into adults with sharp teeth and powerful claws, too much for the owners to handle. There were such raccoons pacing out their lives in separate cages in the neighborhood park near the duplex.

"They'd never make it if we turned them loose," the keeper told Addie when she'd asked about them.

The big moment of the day for those raccoons came when the keeper entered the cages with his rubber boots and hose to spray their concrete runways clean, and then give them dinner in a plastic dog dish. Afterwards they returned to the routine of pace, sleep, pace, sleep, pace. Addie couldn't bear to watch for long.

She couldn't let that happen to Pandora and Prince. Addie picked up Pandora and walked to the door again, a pattern that had become familiar. There was a clattering, and then a bang behind her. She jumped and turned to see Clay dumping a bag of empty tin cans on the floor.

"What are you doing?"

Clay seated himself. He picked up a hammer and nail and then punched a hole in one of the cans before answering.

"I'm getting started on another warning system. We need one. The other got swept away in the flood."

"Oh, Clay, that's a waste of time."

"I don't think so."

"Oh, come on, Clay. If someone can come through rain and flood, they'll come through our little tin-can warning system."

Clay jumped up, his hands on his hips. "Now look here, Adelaide Carver. So somebody saw The Hideaway. They didn't do anything about it, and I say they *aren't* going to do anything about it or it would have happened.

"But what about the others? Honk Groten, we were so afraid of, or Les? Or a bird-watcher, or a flower picker for that matter? We've got to keep up our defense line. I'm not going to quiver here in a corner waiting to be discovered and neither are you. That's not one bit like the Adelaide Carver I know."

Clay finished his speech, keeping his stance for a moment, then he relaxed. "Aw, you know what I mean, Addie. You've been so kind of down — giving up and all."

Addie stood, unmoving. What was that he'd said about *the* Adelaide Carver? She'd never thought of being *the* anyone before.

Pandora squirmed to get loose. Addie

leaned over to set her down on the floor. When she stood up again, her back was ramrod straight.

"You are right, Clay. Just as right as you can be. We've got to do everything we can to stay right here and finish raising these raccoons. Give me that hammer."

Eighteen

Once more the days centered around Pandora and Prince. By the first week in August, Addie had to admit the raccoons were no longer babies but were fast-growing youngsters, already showing the independence, the rebellion, of approaching adolescence.

Prince, now noticeably bigger than Pandora, no longer followed Clay's every footstep, but bounded away up into trees or through logs or down holes, exploring as long as he liked, responding to Clay's call only when he was ready.

Pandora was less exasperating. She had never felt it her duty to respond to Addie's call. Addie was relieved, however, to find that when she removed the collar and leash from Pandora, allowing her to explore freely, she

preferred to stay within view of The Hideaway. Pandora established the branch with the swing on it as her favorite spot. The afternoon sun hit it just right for a sunbath and nap. Sometimes Prince would join her, which was all right with Pandora as long as he didn't crowd into her spot; then, snarling and hissing, she would defend her territory.

The raccoons checked in regularly during the day and always returned by suppertime. They remained affectionate with Addie and Clay, allowing themselves to be scratched behind the ears and cuddled, if only for a moment. Pandora continued to sleep on Addie's bed, even on the hot nights, and Prince continued to ride on Clay's shoulder, although it meant bunching up in order to fit.

Both raccoons began staying awake later at night and sleeping more during the day.

"It's natural," Addie said. "Raccoons are supposed to be nocturnal."

"But I'm not," Clay said.

There was no sleeping in The Hideaway until the raccoons were ready to quit romping, and their romps were longer and more vigorous each evening. Then, toward the end of the second week in August, Prince failed to return for supper.

Clay circled The Hideaway calling until

eleven o'clock before Prince surprised him by springing out of the brush. He ran to Clay and stood on his hind legs, waiting to be picked up.

A few nights later, Prince did not return until morning. Clay couldn't keep from worrying, but Addie assured him, "It's the best thing that could happen. It shows he's really growing up."

"And away from us, I guess," Clay said.

"But, don't you see, that's great! That's just what has to happen. What we *want* to happen," Addie said.

A few nights later, an especially hot night, Pandora refused to come down from her branch in the maple tree. Addie coaxed every half hour until midnight, then finally gave up when Clay reminded her, "It's a good sign. She's growing up."

Addie went to bed, but slept fitfully, getting up several times to make sure Pandora wasn't at the door. Once she slipped outside and discovered Pandora had left the branch. She heard a rustling under The Hideaway. When Addie moved toward it, calling, Pandora galloped away, making it clear she had no intention of being picked up and carried inside.

Early the next morning, Pandora scratched on the screen and waited to be let in. She chirred a greeting to Addie, and after breakfast, curled up to sleep the morning on Addie's bed. But the break had been made.

Addie awoke one morning to a sound that had always made her sad. The woods were filled with the raspy crescendos of the cicadas — locusts, she called them. It was a late-summer sound, the time of the locust, reminding her that it was all coming to an end.

In other years it meant leaving Gram and the farm and going back to the unknown of a new school year. This summer it meant walking away from the raccoons and leaving The Hideaway. Would there ever be another time at The Riffles?

Addie lay in bed allowing herself the comfort of quiet tears. Pandora had nuzzled up to lie beside her. Addie stroked her fur lightly as she looked through blurred eyes at The Hideaway.

It had felt like a great warm nest, holding them all—holding them until they were strong enough to leave. Still, a good nest was meant to be left and this had been a perfect one.

Addie rubbed her eyes dry, grabbed Pandora and pushed the covers aside.

"Hey, Clay, wake up! There are ten days left. Let's not waste a moment of them."

Nineteen

There were seven NO HUNTING signs, fifteen
PRIVATE PROPERTY signs and eighteen ABSO-
LUTELY NO TRESPASSING signs at Groten's.
Addie bought them all.

It might have looked a little strange—Mrs.
Groten almost seemed to smile — but Addie
didn't care. She was going to put the signs up
all over The Riffles — along the fence, along
the river, too, in case some hunter came that
way.

The signs might well get blown down, torn
down or shot up, but she wasn't going to leave
the raccoons at The Riffles without doing everything she could to protect them.

Addie was pleased with the way Pandora

and Prince were maturing. Maybe she and Clay hadn't really taught them anything, maybe it was all instinct, but they could find their own food and shelter and fight, too, when need be.

She was sure they were bigger and heavier than any other raccoons born at The Riffles that year. Certainly no other raccoons were eating whenever they wanted, or had been given both cod-liver oil and a daily treat of children's chewable vitamins. Addie was glad to see the layers of fat on Pandora and Prince. They would be protection against the hungry days of winter.

Except for around their faces, the longer, coarser adult hair had grown to cover most of their soft undercoats. Fat and fur would continue to develop through autumn.

For shelter, both raccoons had poked their noses into enough hollow trees and empty burrows to assure Addie they'd find a suitable home for the long sleeps they would take during the worst of the winter. Clay nailed their den box onto the maple tree and built three more like it to put up in other favorite spots at The Riffles.

Not for one minute did Addie think from the way the two raccoons wrestled, snapped and

snarled at each other, and the way they galloped, climbed and swam, that they couldn't
defend themselves in a normal woodland situation. However, they had been raised by hu-
mans. Hunters might find them easy prey.

"If there were only some way I could be
sure," Addie said. "Most hunters will respect
the signs, but there are always those like Honk
Groten...."

"At least," Clay said, "with all the signs out,
it will look like someone is taking care of The
Riffles."

"I hope so," Addie said. "I hope it looks like
someone is living here."

Addie decided that rather than risk being
seen, she'd wait until after dark to make her
way along the fence line to nail up the signs. It
was Wednesday evening and only once had she
had to pull back into the trees to let the lights
of a car go by. She had one ABSOLUTELY NO
TRESPASSING sign left, and she decided to go
back and put it up across from the farm, in case
Les or anybody else didn't notice the NO
HUNTING sign she'd already nailed there.

She was practicing walking Indian style like
Gram had taught her. Slide one foot in front of
the other. Roll it before putting weight on it,
roll it so that any twigs that might snap or

leaves that might rustle would move with the foot. Addie was concentrating on moving through the woods silently and didn't realize she was actually sneaking up on someone until the voices started. They were just ahead, near the fence. She jumped back in surprise, then froze to listen, her heart pounding.

"What's that? Did you hear that? Something's out there. Honk?"

"Les, cut that out. You're just set on trying to spook me."

"No I'm not. Why would I do that?"

"You want to wiggle out of the deal."

"Nuts, Honk. You're just nuts. I want this cleared up, once and for all. There's something in these woods. I'm not stepping one foot into them, hunting season or any other time, until I know what."

Honk began to laugh, but Les went on.

"You think it's funny, my talking about ghosts and all. Go ahead, laugh. Let's see if you're laughing when you come out of there. You don't get Belle Blue for any measly fifteen dollars until you go to the river and back. And don't forget the sand to prove it."

"I won't forget. I'll get the sand ... and your ghost."

Addie crouched down behind a tree. She

could see Honk bending to slide through the barbed wire. When he stood up again, his flashlight caught the NO HUNTING sign Addie had nailed there less than a half hour before.

"What's this?" Honk turned back slowly to flash the light in Les's face. "Think you're smart, huh? Putting this sign up."

"I...I...didn't," Les whispered. "Honest, I tell you."

"Then who did?"

"I don't know, Honk. Honest. But it's like someone's living here, isn't it?"

Honk turned to flash the light in a circle through the woods ahead. "That's crazy," he said, but no honking laugh followed this time. "I'm going on in," he whispered.

Addie could see him bend down to pick up a long stick. He began thrashing the brush with it and swinging his flashlight from side to side as he moved down the path — the path! Addie stood up. He was going to go right down that path, past The Hideaway on his way to the sandbar!

The raccoons were gone, but Addie had to warn Clay. She'd left him sitting at the table working on their record book. He had the lamp on, the door open...

She'd have to circle and get ahead of Honk.

Somehow she had to warn Clay. Addie put one foot in front of the other, trying to walk silently, yet fast. She was making good time until suddenly she felt a jerk across her shins. *Clank, rattlety, clank* clattered at her feet. She'd stepped into another of the tin-can traps.

Honk called, "Hey, Les. Is that you?" But Les was too far away to hear him.

Addie didn't move until she heard Honk start on again. He was going fast now, like a man anxious to get something over with. At this rate she would not be able to beat him to The Hideaway. If only there were some way to signal...

Once she'd tried to teach Clay how to cup his hands and make the call of the whippoorwill. It was to be their secret warning signal. He hadn't done very well and neither of them had said anything more about it. But there was a chance he'd remember, know something was wrong. They hadn't heard a whippoorwill all summer. Surely he'd notice. He *had* to notice.

"*WoohooHOOOooo. WoohooHOOOooo. WoohooHOOooo. WoohooHOOOooo.*" Addie made the plaintive call, then stopped to listen.

Honk had stopped, too. She waited until he

moved on again. Maybe he was trying to move quietly, but she could hear his every step.

"*WoohooHOOOooo*," she started again, repeating the call eight times without a pause. A real whippoorwill could go on for hundreds of calls without stopping.

Addie zigzagged across the path behind Honk, dropping down to call on first one side and then the other. Surely Clay would hear her and at least wonder why the woods were being invaded so suddenly by so many whippoorwills.

Honk, just ahead, stopped and began thrashing about. Addie could see the light circling and then heard the familiar clattering of pebbles and acorns in tin cans.

"I see you," Honk shouted, and flashed the light up into the trees.

"Playing games, huh?" He turned the beam into the brush at one side and then spun around to the other, shouting, "I've got you."

Honk was turning in a tin-can trap. He didn't think to look at his feet. They were wound in enough string to trip him flat when he tried to step again.

"Who did this?" Honk asked.

"*HOOHOOHOOHOO*," came the answer. An answering sound that made Addie's heart jump, and Honk scramble to his feet. She didn't know what it sounded like to Honk, maybe a dying hoot owl, but to Addie it was music. There was no warble, no vibrato to Clay's version of the secret signal, but it was beautiful. It meant Clay understood!

Honk started slowly, jerkily moving on down the path. Addie hadn't realized they were so close to The Hideaway, darkened as it was, until the woods once more rang out, not with *"Hoo,"* but with *"Ah*'s."

"Ahh - AHHHH - Ah - AHH - AHH - Ah - AHHHHhhhhh."

Addie recognized it at once. Clay made it every time he pushed off on the swing. It was his Tarzan yell. She couldn't see what was happening, but she was sure that a wailing Clay, not unlike a banshee, was swooping out of the darkness at Honk.

The cry faded away. For a moment, the woodlands held silent. Then there was a strained croaking sound, quickly followed by thrashing in the brush and thumping footsteps. It was so sudden, Addie was almost triggered into running herself. But she stood, instead, fascinated by the onrushing figure. Honk was coming full speed, arms and legs pumping and flailing for more speed. He was gasping for breath.

Addie crouched and waited for him to pass.

He was gripping the flashlight, sweeping it rhythmically up and down. As he moved by, it flashed onto his face and off again. But Addie had seen it, a face she'd never forget—the face of a grown man, terrified.

Twenty

If they'd planned all summer, it couldn't have worked out better. Honk tried to deny it, but his mind was set on finding The Riffles haunted, and he had. The NO HUNTING sign, the whippoorwill calls, the clattering of the tin cans, and then finally, coming upon The Hideaway as Clay swung from the tree left no doubt of it. Honk joined Les in spreading the word to stay away from The Riffles, and "Don't ask questions if you know what's good for you."

Clay admitted to Addie that he hadn't intended to swing from the tree. "I slipped," he said. "But when I swing, I yell."

It was more than that. He had been wearing Gram's old yellow slicker.

"I put it on because I thought I'd stick the raccoons in the pockets if I could catch them," he explained.

"Can you imagine what you must have looked like flying out of the night, robes trailing?" Addie laughed. "Poor old Honk."

"Poor old Honk!" Clay looked hard at Addie.

"I feel kind of sorry for him, is all," she explained.

"Sorry for Honk Groten? Boy, Addie, I never thought I'd hear you say that."

"You didn't see his face. He was really scared."

"I just never thought I'd hear you say you felt anything for Honk Groten but hate. Guess after this summer, I shouldn't be surprised at whatever happens."

"It's been something, hasn't it, Clay? This summer. Are you ready to take on the world now?"

"Maybe we can," Clay said, grinning.

The last times for everything began to come. Addie was surprised that she didn't feel as sad as she'd thought she would. The last float trip, the last cleaning of The Hideaway, the last fire in the stove, the last night in the feather beds, the last feeding of the raccoons, the last dishes to be put away and, finally, closing and locking the door—last times never to be forgotten, memories to be stored in their place forever.

Even her last look at Pandora came easier than she'd expected. There were to be no final hugs. Pandora and the Prince were up in the maple tree asleep. She and Clay stood below. They could see the tips of fluffy tails and legs flopped over the branches.

"Sometimes you got to have to leave things you love just 'cause it's best for them, don't you?" Clay said.

Addie put one arm around his shoulders. "Yes, you do, Clay. You most certainly do. But we did all right as parents." She gave him a squeeze. "They'll do all right, too."

"Guess if we can make it, they can," Clay said.

His eyes were full of tears as he picked up the duffel bag and tossed it over his shoulder. Hers were brimful too. She smiled at Clay, not caring that the tears began to spill on down her cheeks. "Let's go, little brother."

"O.K., big sister."

Clay stayed outside to watch for the bus while Addie went into the store. Mrs. Groten came through the curtains at the back as soon as the screen door clicked. She stopped for a moment when she saw Addie. The light was

154

dim, yet Addie was sure the corners of Mrs. Groten's mouth were trying to move into a smile.

Addie picked out candy, gum and some Beef Sticks for the trip. As usual, the transaction was made in silence, but as Addie turned to go, Mrs. Groten said, "Going back now, are you, Adelaide?"

For a moment Addie thought she'd dreamed the words. She turned back slowly to find Mrs. Groten looking right at her. Mrs. Groten's mouth had, indeed, moved into a smile and her dark eyes glistened.

"Wha...what?" Addie stammered.

"Oh, Adelaide Carver, you look too much like your grandmother for me not to know you."

"I...I do? But..."

"I've known all along...since the first day."

"But, why didn't you...?"

"Say anything? I didn't know but that your dad was coming at first. Then, later, I figured it was none of my business to tell as long as you kids were all right. I kept an eye on you."

"*Your* footprints! You came during the flood?"

"And lots of other times."

"Oh, Mrs. Groten, I can't believe it. You've known all summer and we thought it was such a secret!"

"No one else knows," Mrs. Groten said quickly. "I didn't tell Fred Layne even, except that he should keep an eye on The Riffles if he was serious about wanting to catch some law-breaking hunters."

"I just can't believe all this."

"That's not all." Mrs. Groten's smile widened as she reached under the counter and pulled out an envelope. "Got this from your dad this week. Don't know if I should tell, it's his surprise, but then, I guess you might be a little down having to leave and all."

"What is it, Mrs. Groten?"

"Well, your dad says he wants me to check on The Hideaway this winter. Get an estimate on getting it into some sort of shape."

Mrs. Groten stopped to look at Addie. "What kind of shape is it in?"

"Oh, beautiful, just wonderful... but —"

"Now, it says here that your dad's made arrangements not to work next summer. 'Time for me to be with my youngsters,' he writes. 'I want to spend next summer at Addie's place, The Hideaway, she calls it.' "

"Oh, Mrs. Groten!" Addie grabbed her hands and squeezed them, letter and all. "I can't believe it. Wait till I tell Clay." Addie started, then stopped. "Thanks, Mrs. Groten, thanks so much for everything."

156

She hurried to the door, then stopped and turned around.

"Mrs. Groten, there's one thing. About your husband...being so scared at The Riffles. It was us, not ghosts."

Mrs. Groten broke into a laugh that was surprisingly jolly. "I know, Adelaide, all about it. Did you know that prize hound's the pet of a family with four kids over on the other side of the county now? Since all that happened, Honk's been staying pretty close to the store, even helping out some. I don't figure it will do anyone any harm to keep shut about that. Least of all those little raccoons."

Addie gasped. "You know everything!"

Mrs. Groten laughed again. "It's been kind of fun this summer, I'll admit. Thought you might like me to kind of keep an eye on those two raccoons this winter. You know, in case they might have some trouble finding food and all."

"Oh, Mrs. Groten, would you really? Would you really do that? They think they're big, and they are for their age, and really very smart, but they are awfully young. They could use watching over."

"Yes, I know," Mrs. Groten said. "And I do know the way."

Addie laughed with Mrs. Groten this time.

"Hey, Addie—" It was Clay at the door, but even as he called she could hear the sound of the bus approaching.

"I've got to go. Oh, thank you, Mrs. Groten. Thank you for just everything."

Mrs. Groten nodded. "I'll be looking forward to next summer, Adelaide."

"Next summer," Addie repeated. "Next summer at The Riffles. Next summer in The Hideaway." Addie opened the door, then turned back one last time. "And I promise, Mrs. Groten, no secrets next summer."